The Independent Bookworm

ABOUT THE BOOK

Once upon a time in a world where magic and technology collide with unexpected consequences…

Elfin, a male fairy, and Mikael, smith and inventor, want to know what's better, magic or technology. Unfortunately they didn't consider the human factor. Now they have to hurry to save their guinea pig and his loved-ones from the worst, before someone dies.

What if Wilhelm Hauff hadn't realized who was really responsible for „The Cold Heart"?

ABOUT THE AUTHOR

Ever since she was born, Katharina Gerlach had her head in the clouds. She and her three younger brothers grew up in the middle of a forest in the heart of the Luneburgian Heather. After romping through the forest with imagination as her guide, the tomboy learned to read and disappeared into magical adventures, past times or eerie fairytale woods.

She never returned to Earth for long, although she managed to successfully finish training as a landscape gardener, study forestry and gain a PhD. But then, she discovered her vocation: storytelling and realized she'd have to write to make her dream of sharing her stories with others come true.

Katharina loves to write Fantasy, Science Fiction and Historical Novels for all age groups. At present, she is writing at her next project in a small house near Hildesheim, Germany, where she lives with her husband, three children and a dog.

Mehr Informationen: http://de.KatharinaGerlach.com

THE CHALLENGE

THE COLD HEART

TREASURES RETOLD 8

Katharina Gerlach

The Challenge, Treasures Retold 8
published by the Independent Bookworm, USA und D
This book is also available as eBook. It has been published in English and
in German.

If you find any typos or formatting problems in this eBook, please contact
the publisher (www.IndependentBookworm.de).
editor: Ethan James Clarke
printed On-Demand Publishing LLC, 100 Enterprise Way, Suite A200,
Scotts Valley, CA 95066, USA, www.createspace.com

ISBN-13 978-3-95681-073-2

More Information can be found on the publisher's website:
http://www.IndependentBookworm.de

For my family. I couldn't have done it without you.

.

TABLE OF CONTENTS

The Challenge

The coffee is excellent, as always, Elfin thought as he sipped the…
hot brew. After all, Mikael had created the perfect machine for roasting, grinding, and brewing the expensive drink. *He must make a fortune selling those machines to the Southerners.* He had even moved closer to his clients. Thus, Elfin rarely visited his friend these days. The magic he needed for traveling was scarce in the South.

"What's bitten you that you're so quiet?" Mikael set his cup down on the low coffee table, dabbed his blond beard with a napkin, and leaned back, crossing his long legs.

Elfin didn't feel like talking about it, so he filled his mouth with more coffee, before he gazed up at the human.

Mikael grinned. "That bad, ey?"

"All those machines interfere with the land's magic. Most of the South is practically magic free already." Elfin didn't want to start the old argument again, but this time the results affected him directly. "We don't have enough Damsels in Distress anymore. I'm unemployed. Who's ever heard of an unemployed fairy godmother?"

The human laughed. "I guess about as many people as have heard about a male fairy godmother."

"This is not a joke, Mikael. If I don't earn my keep, the queen will question my usefulness and I might lose my job for good." When he set down his tiny cup beside Mikael's, the spoon clattered against the rim. "I love my work and can't imagine doing anything else."

Mikael's smile vanished as if wiped away. "If there's anything I can do to help…"

"You could stop building more and more machines."

"There's no way to stop the advance of technology. We don't need magic for our everyday lives anymore." The human shrugged. "I just don't know how to solve your dilemma."

"Hah!" Elfin jumped up. He barely reached to Mikael's knee. "No need of magic? Who are you kidding? How many Happily Ever Afters have you seen in the South since my kind was driven away? Five? Six? I know the numbers. I keep checking." He balled his hands into fists. "There should have been hundreds. That's what fairy godmothers are for."

"Life is not about Happily Ever After." Mikael's voice was soft, as if he was trying to soften the blow he dealt. "Life goes on and on until we die. There is no perfect point in time, where a human's story ends."

"A Happily Ever After is a beginning, not an end." Elfin didn't expect a human to understand the intricacies of godparenting. "My magic is a tool to help people live a better life."

"As is technology." Mikael frowned and bent forward. "But technology does it on a much bigger scale. With the tools already invented, people don't need to work that hard any more. They will live longer because new ways have been invented to prolong life. We can repair bones or organs that are broken. We can even dampen or enhance emotions if necessary."

"People need magic." Elfin stamped his foot. Unfortunately the red carpet muffled the intended sound completely.

"Sufficiently advanced technology will look like magic to people." Mikael's frown overshadowed his eyes, which made him look dangerous.

"I bet your technology will never be able to provide a single human with a Happily Ever After." Elfin balled his fists and glared at his friend, expecting him to explode. Mikael was a little rash at times. He was rather surprised when his friend leaned back and laughed the roaring, jolly laugh Elfin liked so much.

"A bet. What a splendid idea." Mikael bent forward again and held out his hand. "I accept the bet and will even allow you the first move."

Elfin's jaw dropped, and he needed a little while to recover, but then, he took the offered hand. "Deal. And when I win, you will stop making more machines."

"Deal. But when I win, you will move back here even though there's little magic left in this kingdom."

Elfin agreed. Naturally, he would win. "We'll need a subject in need of a Happily Ever After. Any suggestions?"

"Not a girl. I know that girls are your specialty." Mikael grinned.

Elfin only shrugged. He had worked with boys too. They were a little harder to handle but he'd manage. "Anything else?"

"Well, for obvious reasons, we will have to go to a country with enough magic for you to use." Mikael held his chin with thumb and middle finger and touched his nose with his index finger. "However, if people believe in magic more than in technology, you will have an unfair advantage."

"We could settle on a place that hasn't seen much magic in the last century," Elfin suggested. "I know a couple that have been more or less free of magic users for a while."

Mikael rubbed his hands. "Very well. Get out your crystal ball or whatever else you're using, and let us find a suitable subject."

Pidder stared at his kiln without seeing. In his mind's eye, Lisbeth danced through the woods. Her blond curls sparkled in the few sunbeams than managed to fall through the canopy, and she called him to follow her. It was a wonderful dream.

"Pidder! The kiln." His mother's voice dragged him back to reality. A thick column of black smoke rose from the chimney hole.

"Got it, mother." Hurriedly, he shoveled earth in front of some of the air intake holes at the kiln's base. A few more minutes and the fire would have been so hot, it would have burned the timber to ashes instead of smoldering it into charcoal. When the smoke had turned into a slender column of gray, he went over to where his mother had sat down on a log. She breathed heavily, and the few gray hairs that had escaped the bun under her worn black bonnet stuck to her pale face.

"You must stop daydreaming, Pidder." Although she was scolding him, her eyes rested on him with a look of adoration and love. "We cannot afford to lose a whole kiln."

"I'm sorry. It's so boring here, sometimes." He sat down beside her. "I told you not to come. The path is too steep for a lady."

"I'm not a lady." She slapped his arm playfully, then handed him a piece of black bread the size of her fist. "And I'm not too old to bring lunch to my son if he forgets to take it."

Pidder broke the bread in half and handed one to the old woman at his side. "Have some. It's been a hard climb."

"You will need it to keep up your strength," his mother replied.

"I will not eat if you don't."

They stared at each other silently, a battle of wills, until his mother gave in. She took the offered bread and nibbled on it while Pidder wolfed down his half.

"I found mushrooms." He pointed to a bundle hanging on his staff.

His mother clapped her hands. "I will make us a wonderful soup tonight."

"Better dry them and make the soup some other day." Pidder smiled at her as he got up and grabbed his shovel. "Tonight I'll go to the fair."

Mother's face fell. "Oh, Pidder. Do you really think that's a good idea?"

"I'm going to choke the kiln this afternoon, and it'll need to cool for at least two days before I can open it. It's the perfect time." He went back to work, waving when his mother left with the bundle of mushrooms.

Well before night fell, he returned to their hut that hugged the mountain at the edge of the village. The valley was already dark from the mountain's shadow, and he could see torches somewhere near the fairground. The whole village would be there to make merry even though there wasn't much reason for celebrating. Pidder undressed until he stood shivering in his underpants and pumped water into a bucket. He washed as thoroughly as he could, trying to get the soot out of his hair and skin. He wanted to look his best, just in case Lisbeth noticed him. When he felt clean, he entered the hut, kissed his mother on the cheek and put on his best suit—the one with the brass buttons he had inherited from his late father. The material was a little threadbare at the elbows and knees. He hoped that no one would notice in torchlight.

"The glass factory finally paid for the last coal delivery." Mother handed him another small piece of bread. "I used some of the money to buy more flour. We didn't have any left. I hope you don't mind."

"You know best what we need, Mother." He kissed her once more and left the hut, eating as he hurried down the mountain to the meadow on the other side of the village where the fair would take place. He'd been looking forward to this all summer. Everyone had. Surely Lisbeth would be there. The year of mourning for her mother had been over a couple of months already. Maybe she would even dance. She was so beautiful when she did. If he stood close to the dancefloor, he might be able to watch her.

"Ah, Pidder." Heinrich's heavy hand landed on his shoulder as the owner of the glass factory fell in beside the charcoal burner. "You're just the man I needed to see."

Pidder's heart fell. He hadn't had good news from Heinrich ever.

"You see, my glass factory isn't doing well." Heinrich slurred the words. He smelled of alcohol. "I have to buy my material cheaper, you know? Lower your price somewhat or I'll have to find a different charcoal burner."

"But I'm already working under price, Heinrich. I need the money, or we'll starve."

"When the factory goes down, you won't be earning any money at all, Pidder." The tone in Heinrich's voice made Pidder shiver. If the glass factory stopped producing, most of the villagers would lose their livelihood. *Except Ezekiel*, he thought. The richest farmer in the valley raised cattle and sold the meat in the town at the bottom of the mountain. At least it meant that Lisbeth would not starve.

"Hans from the village on the other side of the mountain already offered me a much lower price." Heinrich held out his hand. "Half price, and you'll stay in the game."

Reluctantly, Pidder took the hand. A little money was still better than none.

They had reached the fairground, and Heinrich left him to sit with Ezekiel. Pidder found a seat close to the dance floor. The music had just started, and the first few couple was walking toward it, when he spotted Lisbeth. Theo bowed to her, and she got up after looking for her father's approval first. From his place, Pidder hat the best view of her slender ankles and swirling skirts whenever she waltzed past him on Theo's arm.

Theo was followed by Hans, Joachim, and Jacob. Lisbeth danced with them all. When she finally returned to her father's table, Pidder gathered all his courage and walked over. Her cheeks were flushed, and she breathed fast. An angelic smile lit her face.

He bowed. "Would you dance with me?" His heart thumped in his throat, and he held his breath.

"I need a little break." She shrugged. "But thank you for asking."

Like a dog that's been kicked in the ribs, Pidder walked back to his place and slumped down on the bench. Why did she dance with every young man in the village but not with him? For the rest of the night, he watched her with burning eyes and a heavy heart. At least she didn't seem to prefer any of the men she danced with. Still, he didn't have the courage to try—and surely fail—again.

○ ○ ○

Elfin materialized at Mikael's side. "I know how to approach him." The luggage horse shied, and Elfin stepped aside so as not to be trampled. "There haven't been any magic operators in recent years, but there used to be a couple of them in that forest. Their legends are still told."

Mikael reigned in his pony and tried to calm the horse he was leading. "Can't you forewarn me? If I lose my luggage, we'll have to go all the way back to fetch new material."

"Sorry." Elfin mounted the horse and whispered into its ear. It calmed immediately. "What I am trying to say is that we can use those legends."

"Tell me about them." Mikael resumed his voyage.

"There's one about a gnome or dwarf or some such." Elfin made himself comfortable on the luggage. "If called with the correct words, he's said to grant three wishes to a Sunday's child."

"Given your size, it's the perfect role for you." Mikael laughed. "Assuming the boy is a Sunday's child."

"I can easily adjust to any size I need. And he doesn't really need to be a Sunday's child as long as he believes he is." Elfin frowned. "Try to take this seriously."

Mikael pulled his cloak closer. "I am taking it seriously, my friend. I'm just cold and hungry."

That, Elfin understood. "We're close to the village already. Soon, we'll need to find a place to stay."

"What about the other legend?" Mikael gazed up at the crowns of the fir trees standing tall as far as the eye can see. "I bet it's got to do with timber. Just tell me I won't have to dress up as a woman."

Elfin tried to imagine his broad-shouldered friend in a dress, the skin on his cheeks still red from shaving off his beard. No way would anyone believe in Mikael if he had to play a woman. Especially since he'd be refusing any magical help. He stifled a giggle. "People tell of a ghost or demon in the shape of a strong man who will take your soul and make you rich if you know how to find him. He's called Lowland Mike."

"What a silly name." Mikael sighed and pointed to a narrow path leading deeper into the forest. "Shall we try that one?"

Elfin nodded and stretched. He'd better scout for a good place to stay.

Mikael turned off the road. "What's yours?"

"My what?"

"Your pseudonym."

"What's in a name?" Elfin prepared to scout ahead.

"Elfin!"

He knew that tone. Mikael would never stop pestering him about the name. He shivered.

"Come on. Is it even sillier than mine?" Mikael beamed at him. "I don't think that's possible."

"I'll be the Glassmanikin." Elfin magiced himself into the forest, but his friend's roaring laugh followed him.

A day later, they had settled in. The cave they had found was spacious and dry, and with Mikael's supplies and Elfin's magic they had made a home out of it.

"It's time to get started," Mikael said. "It's your turn first."

Elfin left their cave and walked closer to the village. When he discovered an elderly woman gathering fallen branches, he made sure that it was the mother of his target. He wove a little spell, sent it into the woman's brain, and her son's birthday appeared in his mind. Elfin calculated. The young man had really been born on a Sunday. What were the odds! Well, it meant he didn't have to lie. He changed his appearance to that of a portly farmer in dark brown breeches, a thick coat, a green vest with silver buttons, and a hat. He even remembered a wet sheen on his forehead. Surely someone with this stature would sweat considering how steep the mountain's flanks were.

"Good day, dear woman." He tipped his hat and bowed slightly. "Do you know your way around here?"

"What if I do?" The woman stood straight, and her eyes examined him warily.

"I am looking for the biggest fir in this part of the forest." He sat on a fallen tree, pulled out a handkerchief, and wiped his forehead.

"What would you need that for?"

"My mother's mother was born in a village nearby. She swore that the Glassmanikin can be found there." He put away his handkerchief. "She even remembered the words needed to call him."

"No one has seen the Glassmanikin in generations." The woman relaxed and took a step closer. "It is said that it will only show itself to Sunday's children."

"I'm aware of that." He smiled at her, and she took another step in his direction.

"You seem rather well off." She pointed at his silver buttons. "What are you going to ask for?"

"My mother, my wife and my daughter are very ill." Elfin pretended to blink away tears. "The Glassmanikin is my last hope if I can find the biggest fir on this mountain."

"I'm sorry to hear that." The woman stepped close to him and put a hand on his arm. "My son will know the way. He is a charcoal burner and knows this mountain better than anyone else. Wait here. I'll fetch him."

"He's not working?"

"His kiln needs to cool, and we had Kirchweih in the village last night. I'll be back in no time."

"I'm coming along." Elfin got up and took the woman's bundle of twigs and branches. "Let me carry this. It's the least I can do."

She allowed it only reluctantly. When they reached her hut, Elfin had to bite his lip. It didn't look fit for living in, but when she called, a young man came out and greeted him. Elfin had seen Pidder in his scrying bowl. In reality, he seemed much bigger with a strong build and curly black hair. The mother explained to her son why Elfin had to find the highest fir in the forest, and soon the two men were on their way. The steeper the ground was, the more Elfin huffed and puffed. He was enjoying his role.

"There it is." Pidder pointed to a massive tree. The trunk was wide enough that three fully grown men wouldn't have been able to embrace it. Elfin was sure that Pidder had found the right tree. With the hollows under its gigantic roots, it suited his plans just fine. With a sigh, he sank down on one of the roots.

"How can I thank you, young man?" He wiped his forehead again.

"May I watch?"

The curiosity in Pidder's voice amused Elfin. The young man was exactly where he wanted him. But he shook his head.

"The supplicant has to be alone." He pretended to shiver. "Alone in a forest like this at midnight. I'm not looking forward to that."

"At midnight?"

"That's what my grandmother said." Elfin magiced two apples into the pockets of his coat, pulled them out and offered one to Pidder. "Want one?"

The young man ate with delight. How little it took to make him happy. Elfin was sure he'd win the bet.

"Are you a Sunday's child?", Pidder asked. Elfin nodded, and Pidder went on. "How does one find out if one is a Sunday's child?"

"Well, your mother should know, shouldn't she? Why don't you ask her?"

"Oh, I don't know." Pidder shook his head but Elfin noticed the excited glimmer in his eyes.

"The most important part is that I use the right words," he said. "My grandmother told them to me when I was a child."

"Can you tell me?"

Elfin smiled. *Yes*, he thought. *Got you.* He stood up. "Why not." He assumed a posture with his hands on his hips and his feet planted slightly apart.

"Treasure Keeper in the forest wild.

Hundreds of years passed by your lands,

the mountain where your fir tree stands.

You'll only appear to a Sunday's child."

He looked at Pidder. The young man's lips moved as he committed the poem to memory. Elfin was actually quite proud of it and looking forward to Pidder's recital. He didn't doubt for a second that the young man would return to the fir tree soon.

Pidder returned to his home three hours after midnight. His mother was still up, worry lines etched into her face.

"Where have you been?" She hugged him.

"I had to wait for him, and then take him to the road into town." Pidder sat down and ate the meager soup she'd prepared for him. It was lukewarm, but he was too tired to wait for her to heat it again. He pulled a silver coin from his pocket and grinned at her. "He paid well though. Says the Glassmanikin granted his wishes. He even sang on the way back."

Mother sat down beside him, took the coin, and bit into it. Since he'd done the same before, he knew it was real. It should last them weeks. Mother sighed.

"He seemed a good man. What a pity he didn't tell you the poem to call the Glassmanikin."

"He did, but what good will it do me? The Manikin will only show himself to Sunday's children." Pidder slurped the last of his soup and wiped his mouth. Maybe they could afford to buy a little meat with the silver coin. Before he could suggest it though, his mother hugged him.

"You were born on a Sunday, Pidder. To this day I hear the church bells drowning out your first cry."

Pidder stared at her open-mouthed. He was a Sunday's child? Why hadn't he known?

"But that means…" His brain took its time adjusting to the news. "It means I can go back tomorrow and ask the Glassmanikin for help myself."

Tears sparkled in his mother's eyes as they sat staring at each other, dumbfounded. Pidder's thoughts were in turmoil. *I can wish for gold and silver, for a house, or enough food for a lifetime, and …* his heart missed a beat. *Lisbeth … Maybe I can ask for her love?*

🔔 🔔 🔔

The next night found Pidder beside the gigantic fir tree in the mountains, huddled into a blanket. Eagerly, he awaited the village church's twelve strokes that announced the midnight hour. They were hard to hear this far from the valley, but if he strained his ears he could just make them out.

Dong, dong, dong …

He folded his blanket and hung it over his shoulder, before he stepped in front of the fir and recited the poem. He felt a little silly. What if the stranger had only made an elaborate joke? No one he knew had ever really met the Glassmanikin.

A warm glow appeared in a hollow under one of the tree roots and a man the size of a fist stepped forward. He wore a silver gown, a silver pointy hat and silver shoes. His silver beard hung down to his knees, and he was frowning.

"Nothing in years and now twice in a row. Have they started breeding Sunday's children just to annoy me?" He glared up at Pidder. "What do you want?"

Pidder bowed deeply.

"I am terribly sorry to disturb you. It's just that I…" His voice faltered.

The Glassmanikin grew a bit and climbed a root to sit on it. He waved to Pidder. "Let's have a look at you, boy."

Pidder bent even deeper.

"Oh, Pidder Munk. Well, well, haven't seen you in a while. Busy chopping up trees, I assume?"

Pidder was too stunned to answer. Of all the people in the village, the Glassmanikin knew him?

"Now, open your mouth and tell me your wishes," the Glassmanikin said. "It's late, and I was on my way to bed."

"I'm sorry," Pidder started again.

"Your first wish, boy." The man tapped his foot.

"I want Lisbeth to fall in love with me." A gigantic stone tumbled off Pidder's heart. There, it was out.

The Manikin shook his head. "I cannot grant you that wish, although I very much approve of your choice of woman. However, love has to be won. It is nothing that magic can provide."

"But how can I win her love if she doesn't even notice me?" Pidder suppressed the tears that threatened to spill.

"You could ask for something that might help her see you for who you are." The Manikin smiled. Suddenly, he looked like an old friend.

Pidder relaxed, and an idea occurred to him. He blurted out. "I want to dance better than all the other boys in the village, and I'd like to have the same amount of money in my pockets as Ezekiel."

The Manikin jumped up and stamped his foot. The gigantic fir tree shivered and rained cones on Pidder. "What a stupid and selfish wish!"

Pidder cowered.

"Unfortunately, I must grant it. That's the rules." The Manikin glared at Pidder. "But I will restrict the wish about the money. You will have as much money in your pockets as Ezekiel, as long as they never fall dry."

Pidder laughed. "Ezekiel always has money in his pockets."

"Well, that's no problem then, is it?" The Glassmanikin stomped his foot again. "Tell me your second wish now. Seeing that you might be stupid enough to waste it too, I will keep the third one for an emergency."

Pidder shivered. His brain worked as slowly as never before. He hadn't thought further than his first wish anyway. What more did one need aside from money and love … the chance at love, to be more precise?

"Well, I haven't got all night." The Glassmanikin was already shrinking again.

"I … I want …" Pidder's brain ground to a halt as it settled on something he could ask for. "I want the glass factory."

"Both wishes are granted. You'll be able to buy the factory tomorrow afternoon." The Manikin glared at him. "You should have asked for brains," he said before he vanished. The glow between the tree roots died.

Trembling, Pidder sat on the ground, thankful that he hadn't wet himself. He even forgot to wrap himself into his blanket again. If he had known how scary the Glassmanikin could be, he would have thought twice before coming here. His fingers were so cold, he shoved them into his pockets. What was that? He pulled out something round, a coin, and examined it. Gold! This was a gold coin. Could it be? He bit into the coin and felt his teeth sink into the soft material. Yes, it was true. He really had as much money as Ezekiel. *Mother and I will never starve again.* Still trembling, Pidder laughed.

"That went well." Mikael forced himself not to laugh. His friend was agitated enough as it was.

"Why did that idiot have to ask for something so stupid?" Elfin paced to and fro in the kitchen in their cave. "Doesn't he have a brain?"

"I'm sure he has. But midnight … a dark forest … and a magical man the size of a fist that can make the biggest tree of the forest tremble…" Mikael bit his lip and breathed deeply before continuing. "Those are probably not the best circumstances for thinking clearly."

Elfin stopped his pacing and glared at his friend.

Mikael still felt the tickle of laughter inside but he tried to stay as serious as he could. "Would you like some coffee?"

"Very well." Elfin disappeared and reappeared beside his chair which stood on the table. "Don't forget, it's your turn next. I'm really curious to see what you have planned."

Mikael filled Elfin's small cup with coffee, picked up his own, and sipped before answering. "Before that, I'm curious to see what Pidder will do with your gifts. Shall we watch him?"

Elfin visibly relaxed as they turned to the scrying bowl.

Pidder slept through the whole morning and was still tired when he sat down for lunch. How would he go about buying the glass factory? He decided to go to the village inn to see if he could talk to Heinrich. Recently, the current owner had been spending a lot of time there.

He entered the inn and ordered a glass of beer before he searched the room for Heinrich. He wasn't there, but Ezekiel, a rich farmer, and a timber merchant sat at a table in the corner playing cards. Ezekiel won, wiped the coins from the table, and put them into his pocket.

Pidder's hand flew to his own pocket. It had become heavy with money. Not daring to breathe, he picked up his beer and slipped into a seat at a corner table out of sight of the others. He pulled out the money and began to count, but the voices at his back disrupted his concentration.

"How long are they going to keep him?" the timber merchant asked.

"For an eternity, methinks." Ezekiel chuckled. "No one in his right mind would buy his glass factory."

"People in town don't pay well for glass any more. Trumps." A slap indicated that the farmer had laid a card onto the table.

"Oh no … not heart." The salesman sighed. "So, if someone buys his factory, he'll be a free man again?"

"There's no reason to keep him if his debts are paid," Ezekiel said. "That one's mine."

Another slap and a groan from the timber merchant followed.

The factory is for sale! Pidder marveled at the ingenuity of the Glassmanikin. Now all he needed was enough money for a down payment. He ignored the gamblers and concentrated on counting his money. Two hundred and three gold coins and a handful of silver. Pidder was dumbfounded. This was more than enough. How could Ezekiel run around with that much money in his pocket? Shouldn't he lock it in a strongbox or hide it?

In a hurry, he wrapped the coins into his handkerchief, hid the bundle under his threadbare jacket, approached the gamblers, and greeted them.

"I couldn't help but overhear your conversation," he said. "If someone was interested in buying the glass factory, where would he have to go?"

"You're interested in the factory, Pidder Munk?" Ezekiel laughed out loud. "I don't think you've got enough money."

The farmer nodded gravely. "They'll want a down payment of at least a thousand and five hundred silver coins."

"I'm just curious." Pidder tried to be non-committal. "If someone would like to help Heinrich, where would he go?"

"To the debtor's prison in town, of course." The timber merchant waved to the last empty chair at the table. "Care to join us?"

"He can't."

"I can't."

Pidder and Ezekiel spoke in unison.

"I've got work to do," Pidder continued. He said his farewell and left the inn. Straight-backed, he turned toward the town. It was half a day's walk either way but the thought of owning a glass factory drove him onwards.

As the proud owner and with a copy of Ezekiel's riches in his pockets, Pidder changed a couple of things in the glass factory over the next three months. His first decision was to pay the charcoal burners higher prices. Also, he reduced the time workers had to spend at the ovens, and he developed glass ornaments like silvered fir tree cones for Christmas. He had a bigger timber frame house built, and moved in with his mother, marveling at how fast these things could be done with enough money. He enjoyed being the center of attention even though Ezekiel always taunted him, suggesting he stole his money or earned it with smuggling. Pidder kept his secret.

In his free time, of which he had a lot now, he organized weekend dances which made him very popular with the village's young inhabitants, with the innkeeper, and with Lisbeth. His body filled with joy whenever he danced with her, and due to his new abilities and nicer clothing, he soon became Lisbeth's favorite dancing partner.

On a rainy Friday in October, the glass merchant arrived to look at Pidder's wares.

"What are these?" He pointed at the silvery fir cones, the colored glass balls, and the glass angels.

"Christmas ornaments."

"No one's going to pay a dime for those," the merchant said.

"People will love them." Pidder pulled out his watch to see how much time he still had before the dance. "They need something more than apples and straw stars to hang up in their Christmas trees."

"They need bottles and vases and drinking glasses, but not this…" The merchant flipped his hand. "This childish nonsense."

Pidder shrugged. "If you're not interested, I'll sell them myself."

"Good luck with that." The merchant returned to his cart and left.

Good riddance. After all, I don't need his money. Pidder sighed with relief. He wouldn't be late. In his mind he saw nothing but Lisbeth's pair of brown eyes, and her rosy cheeks flushed with the excitement of the dance.

When the evening drew to a close, Pidder took Lisbeth's arm, led her out of the inn and across the street to her father's house.

"Thank you for a wonderful evening again, Pidder." She smiled up at him, and his throat constricted. Unable to talk, he simply nodded. "You know, I like it that you're not as stingy as my father."

"Your father just knows better how to keep his money together." This was safer ground. He tried to smile too but failed miserably. All he wanted to do was tell her how much he loved her, and instead he uttered banalities about her father. "If you don't mind, I will pick you up next Friday again."

"I do mind."

Pidder's heart missed a beat. What had he done wrong? Why wouldn't she want him to pick her up again? Before he could clear his throat to ask, she grabbed the lapels of his coat and pulled him toward her until their lips met. She tasted of apple juice and took Pidder's breath away.

Releasing him, she said, "Come back first thing in the morning."

"Lisbeth," he breathed.

"Pidder." She giggled. "You can be so slow sometimes. I've been in love with you since forever."

At this revelation, Pidder's heart widened, but a splinter of doubt remained. "Why did you refuse to dance with me then, when I was still poor?"

"My father forbade it. I wasn't allowed to dance with anyone who didn't at least have a certain amount of money." Lisbeth sighed. "Most of the time that was no problem. The poorer men hardly ever approached me. You were the only one who never gave up. God, how it hurt to see the look in your eyes when I refused yet again." She put her arms around him, and he shivered with happiness.

Regions of his body began to stir that had no right to be moving outside a marital bed.

"I love you more than my own life." His voice was hoarse.

"It's written all over your face." She kissed him again. "I want you to talk to my father soon."

Before he could say more, she kissed him a final time and ran inside, leaving him behind with trembling knees. He had to hold on to the wooden fence to keep from falling. *Thank you Glassmanikin*, he thought. *All my dreams are coming true.*

"It seems like things are turning out well for our subject," Elfin said. "I told you that a Happily Ever After could only be achieved by magic."

"He isn't married yet." Mikael frowned at his friend. "And he took more than three months to get to this point."

"True." Elfin stretched. "We'll have to find you a new test subject after Pidder's wedding to see if you can do it faster."

"As I said, he's not married yet." Mikael stood up and turned off the light. "Let's call it a day."

❍ ❍ ❍

Early in the morning, Pidder washed thoroughly, shaved, and donned his Sunday best. Not the old suit he had inherited from his father, but a brand new set of clothes that he had ordered in town. HE had even squandered money on linen undergarments.

"Oh, you look smart this morning." His mother smiled at him.

"I will ask Ezekiel for Lisbeth's hand today. Wish me luck." Unable to eat, he kissed her cheek and left their new house. He didn't have far to go. It was very early in the morning, so he was quite surprised to see the reeve approach him. The little village's man for all police and administrative works wore his usual frown.

"Morning, Pidder." The gaunt man put a hand on his shoulder. "The town bailiff contacted me. You forgot to pay your second installment for the glass factory."

"I'm sorry, reeve." Pidder had to force himself to turn his thoughts away from his endeavor. The installment had completely slipped his mind. He put his hands into his pockets and pulled out what money he had. "Here is a partial payment. I have more, but I have to talk to Ezekiel first."

"This should do, but I really need the rest by tomorrow latest." The reeve pocketed the money. "What do you want with the old nickel nurser?"

Pidder blushed. "Lisbeth told me to ask him for his permission to get married."

The reeve laughed. "Well, boy, good luck with that. Ezekiel has always wanted someone special for his daughter. For your happiness, I hope you're it."

"I'm as rich as he is." Pidder stood straight. "I should suit him fine."

"As I said, good luck." The reeve turned and walked away, leaving Pidder to his thoughts.

I will marry Lisbeth, one way or another, he swore to himself and walked into the yard of Ezekiel's farm house. The rich farmer was still asleep. Settling down on a chair in the house's kitchen area, he watched Lisbeth direct the maids. She looked like a queen to him. Soon, the smell of porridge and herb tea filled the house, and Ezekiel left his bedchamber, yawning and stretching. Pidder had to bite his lip to keep from laughing. With his white nightshirt and thin legs, the portly man looked like a giant white spider—minus a few legs, of course.

"Oy, neighbor. You're up early." Ezekiel turned back to his bedchamber. "I'll be with you in a minute. Let me just get dressed."

When he returned, he led Pidder into the good room where he settled into a comfy chair beside the iron oven. He didn't ask Pidder to sit.

"What can I do for you?" He stuffed his meerschaum pipe.

"As you might have noticed, I have come into money recently." Pidder wiped his wet palms off on his trousers and tried to calm his speeding heart. "So, I would like to ask you for Lisbeth's hand in marriage."

"Forget it." The pipe lit and Ezekiel vanished behind a cloud of smoke.

"But I have as much money as you have."

"That's not the point. I've had requests from people richer than you are." Ezekiel puffed some more. "None of them was good enough for my daughter, and neither are you. We'll wait for a baron or a prince."

"Lisbeth and I are in love." Pidder clenched his fists. He had to convince the old man.

"What's love got to do with it? You're not good enough, and that's that." Ezekiel leaned back and folded one leg over the other. "Now, leave me."

Pidder bit his tongue and fought hard not to attack the stubborn man. That'd ruin any chance he might still have. "Your daughter will die a spinster. No prince or baron has ever come this way."

"Mind your own business."

Pidder turned and stormed out of the room. He stumbled right into Lisbeth, who'd been waiting for him. She grabbed his hand, pulled him over to the big table where the farm workers usually had their breakfast, and they sat.

"I feared he'd say no," she said, biting back tears.

"There must be a way." Pidder stared at the table, unable to bear the sadness on her face. "If only I could bribe him or force him."

"Pidder, you're a genius." Lisbeth put her hand on his arm and bent forward. "Remember how proud he is that he always keeps his word?"

Pidder nodded.

"Have you noticed how much he loves to gamble?" Her eyes sparkled.

When her meaning and what that suggested for him dawned on Pidder, his jaw dropped. It took him ages to recover, but then he shook his head. "I can't do that. I'd lose too much."

"It'd be for me." Lisbeth cocked her head and fluttered her lashes at him. "Don't you think that's worth the risk?"

"What if I end up a beggar again?" Pidder held his breath. He knew it was a possibility.

"I will always love you, money or not." The words were uttered quietly, yet with a sense of iron behind them. Pidder's heart thumped. If *she* was willing to risk this, so would *he*.

"I'll do it." He pushed himself up and walked back to the good room.

"What do you still want?" Ezekiel glared at him.

"Let's play a game of cards or," he halted, "a game of dice."

The old man's eyes lit up. "You're willing to play?"

"My fortune against her hand in marriage." Pidder wanted to bite back the words but knew he couldn't.

"I'll add the money in my pockets as a dowry into the bargain." Ezekiel took the pipe out of his mouth, got up and held a hand out to Pidder. "This afternoon, three a clock in the inn."

With sagging shoulders, Pidder went home. He hated gambling, and now he was forced to do it.

"What happened?" His mother took his hands and gazed into his eyes with a worried frown on her face. He told her everything.

"I might lose it all," he finished.

"I am not afraid of that. We've been poor before. If it gives you a chance at happiness, I'll gladly risk being poor again. We managed before, and we'll manage after." She squeezed his hands.

Pidder blinked back tears. She was right, but he'd better be prepared. With a sigh, he pulled as much money from his coat as he could find in its pockets. It wasn't much. Obviously, Ezekiel hadn't yet refilled his pockets. But it should be enough to get them through a couple of weeks if bad came to worse.

Duly at three a clock, Pidder entered the inn. Ezekiel was already there, as was every man in the village. Had the miser really spread the word? Pidder's ears went hot. This was a business between the two of them. Why would he want this many witnesses?

"Is it true?" The farmer who usually played with Ezekiel tugged at his sleeve. "You're going to play a round of dice against him?"

Pidder nodded.

The farmer bent forward. "Make sure he's not cheating. He's good at that, especially if he's got a lot to lose."

"Thank you for the tip." Pidder squeezed through the crowd toward the table.

"I didn't think you'd come," Ezekiel said. "The two best throws?"

"Fine with me." Pidder sat down. He turned to the crowd gathered around them. "Did he tell you all why I'm doing this?"

Stunned silence.

Then the farmer asked, "There's a reason for your change of mind?"

"That's none of your business," Ezekiel interrupted. He slammed a pair of dice onto the table. "Let's get started."

He doesn't want them to know! A smile grew on Pidder's face.

"I'm not a gambler," he said. "Therefore, I want the rules and the stakes to be clear. We will throw the dice as often as necessary and the first one with two winning throws will become the overall winner, right?"

"Yes." Ezekiel's hand trembled slightly as he pointed to the chair opposite him. "Now, sit down."

But Pidder wasn't thwarted. "If you win, you will get my money, the glass factory, and everything else I own. If I win, I will get Lisbeth's hand in marriage."

A collective gasp went through the crowd. Ezekiel ground his teeth.

"No need to shout if from the rooftops."

Pidder sat down and took the dice. He shook them gently in his hand, then handed them to Ezekiel. "You first."

The merchant glared at him, but took the dice without hesitating. He held them in both hands and shook them for a moment, then threw them on the table. They rolled a little. Everybody was holding their breath.

Twelve.

Before Ezekiel could pick up the dice and hand them to Pidder, the young man had grabbed them. Their weight was off. He smiled inwardly. Without much shaking, he rolled them over the tabletop.

Twelve.

"We need new dice," he called to the innkeeper and slammed his hands over the ones on the table. "There's something strange about these ones."

"Are you accusing me of cheating?" Ezekiel half rose off his chair.

"Not at all." Pidder smiled but his eyes remained cold. "But this is the most important game I will ever play, so I need to be certain, that we have the same chances of winning."

"Fine." Ezekiel sank back down and waited for the innkeeper to bring new dice, but Pidder could hear the anger in his tone.

He hoped that Ezekiel only had a single pair of manipulated dice. They must have cost him a lot of money. They got the new dice, and this time, Pidder threw first.

Eight. Not bad, but not really good either.

Ezekiel threw a six and a three.

Pidder swallowed and took the dice again. *Please Glassmanikin, help me.*

The dice rolled over the table. Eight.

Ezekiel laughed and threw. Five. He swore.

Again they threw the dice. Six for Pidder; six for Ezekiel. Despite the many people in the inn, no sound could be heard aside from breathing.

Pidder's mouth tasted like he'd eaten a rotten apple, and he felt parched when he took the dice again. He closed his eyes and breathed deeply. *Please, let me win this round.*

The dice rolled over the table top, one teetering dangerously close to the edge before settling down. Ten. Pidder didn't dare to hope.

Ezekiel picked up the dice with trembling fingers. He shook them in his hands for what seemed to be an eternity before dropping them onto the table. The first one stilled after toppling a few times. Six. The second one spun much longer. When it finally settled, it showed a three.

Pidder slumped. He hadn't even noticed that he'd been holding his breath.

Ezekiel sat motionless. His face was pale as death, and his gaze fixed on the dice.

"I ... I lost." His voice was barely more than a whisper.

"You lost." The farmer laughed. "For the first time in an eternity, you lost, Ezekiel!"

The inn erupted into roaring laughter.

Invigorated by the thought of how happy Lisbeth would be about the news, Pidder stood up. "We will get married next Sunday, before you can come up with another scheme."

"The dowry," the farmer shouted.

"The dowry, the dowry, the dowry," the rest of the crowd fell in.

With trembling knees, Ezekiel got up and began to empty his pockets. Pidder would have loved to leave the money and run to his beloved, but the crowd wouldn't let him through before he pocketed the last coin from the table. He barged through the men toward the door, and everyone slapped his shoulders or back, congratulating him. When he finally broke free, he hurried toward Lisbeth's home. *I won! I haven't lost everything to Ezekiel.* His heart began to skip in the rhythm of his feet. *Lisbeth will be my wife.*

Too happy to comprehend his luck, he shoved his hands into his pockets.

They were empty.

The Glassmanikin's voice echoed through his head. *You will have as much money in your pockets as Ezekiel, as long as they never fall dry.*

His heart plummeted. How would he pay the rest of his debts now? *I must talk to the Glassmanikin again. He has to give me enough money so I can provide a comfortable life for Lisbeth and Mother. If I leave before nightfall, I should be able to get to his fir before midnight,* he thought. Thankful that it was time for the full moon again, Pidder hurried on. At least he had Lisbeth. The rest would follow, he was sure.

◐ ◑ ◐

"See, I told you he hasn't reached his happy end yet." Mikael sat up from the scrying bowl and pointed to the young man's empty pockets. "You know what? I should invent something like your bowl for everyone. Imagine if it was possible to watch your loved ones over a distance and maybe even talk to them. That'd be quite the invention."

"Stop your sidetracking," Elfin said. "I'll have to think about what to tell him when he shows up again."

"Nothing. It's my turn now." Mikael got up and fetched himself a cup of coffee, leaving Elfin to watch the young couple embrace in the yard of Lisbeth's father's house.

"But he's still got one wish left."

"True enough." Mikael sipped. "However, with the emotional turmoil in his heart, he'll choose something as foolish as the rest. Give me a chance."

Elfin considered this for a while, then nodded. "You're right. Try it and we'll see."

Mikael looked around the cave. The cold walls and the ground were covered with carpets. Comfortable chairs, a bookshelf, a table, two differently sized beds, and a fireplace completed their home. "This looks far too cozy," he said. "I'll need something that resembles a workroom."

"Well, since this is your part of the game, I won't magic it here for you." Elfin folded his hands over his belly and grinned.

"No need." Mikael put down his cup. "I brought all I'll need with me." He left the cave. After all, there were many more nearby.

◌ ◌ ◌

A few hours later, he sat on a stone close to a gorge Pidder would have to cross to reach the fir tree. Night had already fallen. The trees stood like tall, dark soldiers behind him. To impress Pidder, Mikael had sewn tiny lightbulbs powered by tamed lightning to the inside of his collar. He hid the miniature steam engine necessary to produce the tamed lightning in a pipe. The greenish light illuminated his bearded face from below. Mikael thought he looked intriguing. All in all, he was quite proud of the effect.

When he noticed a shadow moving through the trees toward the gorge, he hid behind a tall stone. He didn't want to give Pidder the chance of turning back. The young man passed his hiding place a little later, and Mikael stepped out.

"Good evening, Pidder Munk," he said.

Pidder spun round, and his jaw dropped.

"So, are you on your way to El…, ehm … the Glassmanikin again?"

"How do you know?" Pidder took a step backward.

"I'm a knowledgeable man, Pidder." Mikael smiled. "I also know about your troubles."

"I'm not in trouble." Pidder took another step backward.

Mikael began to suspect that illuminating his face from below probably hadn't been the best idea after all. *Maybe I should have worn a hat.* He smiled some more. "I can help you to keep your glass factory. If you work a little on your distribution you should be able to offer Lisbeth an adequate lifestyle. The idea with the Christmas tree ornaments was brilliant."

Pidder stepped forward. His face shone. "Do you really think so? Everybody laughed at the idea."

"All you need is a little money to pay for proper distribution and some business sense." Mikael held out his hand. "By the way, they call me the Lowland Mike."

"Lowland Mike." Pidder paled. "I'm not going to give you my soul."

"Is that what they say about me? That I'm stealing souls?" Mikael's eyes widened. That cheating pipsqueak … That'd teach him to trust Elfin in a competition again. He straightened. "Well, they're very wrong. What would I do with souls?"

"Why are you offering to help me then?" Pidder stood rooted to the spot, but seemed brave enough to at least stay and listen. "What will you get if you do?"

"I've got a little bet running with the Glassmanikin that I'd like to win," Mikael said. "Why don't you listen to my idea. If you don't like it, you can always leave."

Pidder watched him silently, pondering the offer.

"I can give you both, money and a level head." Mikael held out his hand once more.

A barely noticeable jerk went through Pidder, and he took it. "But if I don't like your suggestion, I will need to call the Glassmanikin before midnight."

"That should not be a problem. My home is near enough. You can be at his fir tree in ten minutes from there." Mikael led the way. They walked in silence. Only when they reached the cave he had chosen for his part of the charade, did Pidder speak again.

"I've never seen this cave before, and I know this forest like the pocket of my coat." His gaze traveled over the bare walls, the stones Mikael had hollowed and illuminated from the inside, the stone bench that had been made to look like a bed, the tools hanging on one of the walls, and the piles of gold, silver, brass and iron stacked on a stone shelf beside one of Mikael's coffee makers.

"Not all things are always visible," Mikael said. "Would you like some coffee?"

"Ehm ... yes?"

Mikael knew that Pidder didn't know what that was, and he admired his love of adventure. He filled two cups and sat down on a chair beside a stone that served as a table. He pointed to a second chair. "Make yourself comfortable."

Pidder sat and sipped. His eyes widened, and his mouth twisted.

"Do you like it?"

"Ehm, it's interesting." Pidder set the cup down and leaned forward ."What is your idea then?"

"I've been watching you for a while now and found that your decisions are always based on how you feel." Mikael scratched his beard. "I invented something that will siphon off your emotional spikes and turn you into a level headed young man. With your natural intellect and less erratic behavior, you should be able to make your fortune."

"That sounds interesting. How would you do it?"

"I've found that the key to controlling emotions is a manipulation of hormone levels. My invention will be two small gadgets..."

"I've never been to university," Pidder interrupted him. "Can't you explain it in a way that I can understand?"

"Fine." Mikael understood why Elfin was a little miffed after his encounter with Pidder. He was annoyed too. The best part of an invention had always been when he could explain it to a user. Obviously, this user wasn't really interested. He could as well make up a magical tale. "You could say that I'm going to take your heart and replace it with a stone."

"But I'll die without my heart."

"No, you won't. The stone will work just like your heart." Mikael had an idea. He pointed to the hollowed stones that shone from the inside with a reddish light. "See those?"

Pidder nodded.

"They belong to Ezekiel, the town's bailiff, and a baron or two." Mikael grinned. Making up a story was much more fun than he had expected. "They're all still alive."

"So, you'd give me a heart of stone that will make me more level headed?" Pidder cocked his head but frowned. He obviously needed some more convincing.

"And you can take half of the pile of gold you see over there." Mikael pointed to his precious metals. Sure, half of the pile was a lot of money, but he could afford it.

Pidder's face lit up. "In that case, I'm in."

"I didn't expect anything else." Mikael said, and caught Pidder's body as it slumped. *Considering that Pidder only had a single sip of the coffee, I've probably overdosed the sedative. Working with people seems more difficult than working with machines.*

After covering the stone that served as a table with a sheet he had sterilized at home, Mikael laid Pidder very gently on top of it, then put away the cups. He scrubbed his hands with alcohol until they smarted. Then he fetched the tools he would need. He had cooked them for hours before packing them for the trip. He knew hoe easily a wound infected without this precaution, so he double-checked that they were spotlessly clean and sterile.

It just won't do to harm the patient, he thought as he sliced through Pidder's skin on his thigh with a scalpel. A tiny gap opened and blood welled out. Mikael put some cotton around it to keep it from dripping on the sheet. Luckily he didn't need a big cut to feed his placement gadget into Pidder's body.

Very carefully, he eased the tube with the first gadget through the veins until he felt the puckering heart in his fingers. *That's close enough.* He pressed a button that would release the gadget. It would then attach itself to the vein automatically. Once the tube had left the body and the wound was dressed, Mikael sighed with relief although this had been the easy part. Next, he needed to place a second filter drone close to the brain.

He had studied several possibilities to get close enough and had settled on the jugular. The cut here needed to be even smaller to prevent too much blood from spilling. Mikael worked with great care. Once the tube was inserted, the blood flow stopped. Very, very carefully, he maneuvered the tube upwards. He had to guess at the best place to drop the filter, but once it was released, it would sit in the wall of the vein doing its job for as long as it could siphon sugars from the bloodstream and convert it into energy.

Mikael removed the tube as gently as he had pushed it in. Then he stitched the tiny wound with one of Pidder's hairs and a sterile needle. The young man would probably not even notice he'd been operated on, not by the wounds at least. Naturally he would notice that the two filters in his bloodstream are reducing the surplus of hormones in a way that would make him much more rational.

Mikael put half of the gold he had brought into a money pouch and put it into Pidder's pocket. Then he picked up his patient and carried him carefully to the gorge where he laid him on a bed of moss before he returned to the cave, pulling a big stone back in front of the entrance. *That was a job well done*, he thought, before going to bed.

❁ ❁ ❁

"What a strange dream," Pidder said, and sat up. Gingerly, he touched the ache at the side of his neck. Something must have bitten him during the night. He looked around. Where was he? He adjusted his coat and noticed something quite heavy in his pocket. When he looked, he found a purse filled with gold. A bolt of elation shot through him but soon subsided.

Oh, he thought. *So it wasn't a dream after all. That should be enough to pay for my glass factory.* But instead of feeling elated and happy about the unexpected wealth, he shrugged and pocketed it again. *I'd better go home or Lisbeth will worry.* He yawned and got up, wondering why the thought of Lisbeth didn't make his heart race. After all, he had won the right to marry her. Hadn't that been his heart's desire? Shouldn't it be racing with joy? The memory of a voice surfaced.

"You could say that I'm going to take your heart and replace it with a stone."

Pidder shrugged again. Obviously, Lowland Mike had made good on his end of the bargain. Fine. He really did feel a lot more level headed. He'd travel into town and pay his dues, and then he'd get the wedding organized and find a couple of people to sell his glass ornaments in town. With a head this calm, it should be easy to set everything in motion.

A few hours later, he returned to his village after he had gone into town to pay all outstanding installments for the glass factory. Lowland Mike had given him enough money, and now Pidder was the full owner. Immediately, he hired three men to carry baskets of Christmas ornaments on their backs into the kingdoms and bigger towns to sell. The idea left him strangely unsatisfied. As if something was missing. Well, at least Lisbeth would not have to live in his mother's old hut after the marriage. She had been so happy when he told her about her father's permission and had agreed that they had to act fast before Ezekiel reneged on his promise. He had felt a prick of happiness at her shining eyes. But it was gone as fast as it had come, as if someone had wiped it away.

Over the next few weeks everything went as he had planned. Even Ezekiel grudgingly accepted him as a son-in-law. However, the joy he had hoped to gain did not appear. Sure, he felt tiny pangs of pride and happiness when he watched Lisbeth prepare food or when he watched her sleep beside him, but most of the time, he only felt lethargic. Uncaring, Pidder returned from work in the evenings; uncaring, he ate the excellent meal his wife had prepared; uncaring, he spent time in the company of his father-in-law, and, uncaring, he got up in the morning and returned to work. One day flowed into the next with nothing to distinguish them.

"I'm not at all sure this was such a good idea," Elfin said, looking up from his scrying bowl. "There seems to be something wrong with him."

"Nonsense. He's got more money than ever before, and what's more, he earned it through his own talent." Mikael stepped beside his friend and looked over his shoulder at Pidder, who lay on the sofa in the good room, the house's formal living room, snoring gently.

"But I haven't seen him smile once in the last two weeks. He didn't even dance much at his own wedding."

"Well, he did drink quite a lot, didn't he?" Mikael smiled. "Believe me. He's happy."

"I will need to hear that from his own lips."

"You're just too jealous to admit that I've won the bet," Mikael said.

"I no longer care who won." Elfin pulled at his hair. "I'm truly worried about him."

Mikael sat down beside his friend and bent forward. "I might not understand why you're so scared, but I'm willing to find out. Let's watch him for a few days and nights. I'll take the first shift."

Elfin looked up at him. "Thank you, Mikael."

Pidder walked into the kitchen later than usual. Lisbeth wasn't in sight, but his mother was sitting beside the hearth, stirring the pot. When she saw her son, a worried frown crossed her features.

Nodding toward her, Pidder slumped on his chair, pulling the bread closer. He wasn't all that hungry, so one slice with a little butter would be enough.

His mother came over and sat on a chair beside him.

"Pidder, what's wrong with you? I've never seen you like this before." She put her hand on his arm.

"Nothing." Pidder wasn't in the mood for talking. He wanted to feel something, anything.

"Is there anything I can do to help you?" The worry lines on his mother's face annoyed Pidder. Why couldn't she just leave him alone? A deep sadness filled his heart. Pidder struggled to keep the feeling, but it vanished like snow in the sun.

"I need to be alone for a while." He got up without finishing his bread and left the house. Something was missing from his life and he wanted to know what. He needed to get it back. Struggling to keep his determination, he walked toward the glass factory with long strides. A horse whinnied. He turned and saw a rider gallop through the little village. The horse's eyes were bloodshot and the man clung to the mane, screaming for people to get out of the way. Pidder was able to identify the panic in his voice but it left him unmoved. Like a tree, he stood in the middle of the road watching the horse careen toward him. It grew in size in mere seconds. The man's screams became more urgent. And Pidder felt.

Fear shot through his veins. His heart hammered in the rhythm of the horse's hooves that came bearing down on him. Warm wetness was running down his legs.

At the last possible moment, he stepped aside, grinning with delight, and grabbed the reins. The panicked horse ripped him off his feet and dragged him along. Pain rippled through his legs where they scraped over the ground, and his arms ached from holding up his weight as best as possible. The horse turned to the side he clung to. It slowed, trotted, and finally stood.

Pidder staggered to his feet. Elation filled him, and he grinned from ear to ear. That was what had been missing form his life. Excitement!

The man on the horse turned out to be the new vicar from town who had come to get to know his congregation. As he thanked Pidder for his rescue over and over again, the familiar numbness enveloped Pidder. He shrugged and accepted the praise stoically. Then he left the village.

The factory can look after itself for a day, he thought as he walked into the forest.

Soon he arrived at the gorge where he had met Lowland Mike. It wasn't a very big gorge as gorges went, but it was wide enough that jumping it would be a challenge. Pidder stepped right to the edge and stared down. His heart began to race, and he felt fear rise in his throat. If he fell in …

What a feeling! He smiled and took a step back. Finally his heart was waking up again. He took a few more steps back and catapulted himself forward. At the edge of the gorge, he pushed hard, flying toward the other side, screaming his joy and fear into the cold autumn air.

He slammed into the ground, laughing like mad. He made it alive, and he felt. Before the numbness could return, he jumped again … and again … and again. When he was too exhausted to try it once more, he turned back toward the village. A few minutes later, the now familiar numbness of not feeling anything returned. *I'll need to do that more often*, he thought. *It might be dangerous but I feel so alive.*

When he reached his house, one of the men he'd sent out to sell his wares was waiting for him. He handed Pidder a fat purse and the notebook with the list of what he'd sold to whom at what price.

"People have gone crazy over your ornaments," the seller said, his face shining with delight. "We need to make more as fast as we can."

Pidder wished he could be as happy as this man. But even the longing didn't last for more than a split second.

"I'll see to it." He pulled out his own purse and handed the man a silver coin. "Go home and relax until we have more wares."

The man danced away.

Pidder felt the weight of the purse he held. It was surprisingly heavy. Maybe it held more than copper coins. He went into the good room of his house and emptied it on the table. A small mountain of silver and gold coins sparkled in the light that fell through the glass windows. He gasped. *They're mine. They're all mine.* His heart started racing. *So much money.* He'd never seen this much minted money in one place in his whole life. *Ezekiel will pale with jealousy when I show him.* His hands shook as he sat down to count the sparkling coins. It occurred to him that Ezekiel might want a share if he knew how much money Pidder had made with his ornaments. Hurriedly, he slipped the money back into the purse, except for a few silver coins, and searched for a good hiding place. In the end, he put it into a big wooden box in the corner. *I'll need to get a lock for it or someone might steal it.* When he wiped his sweaty palms on his pants, he realized that he was still feeling excited and happy. So it was possible to feel something without facing danger. *I'll need to earn more, much more.* He put the remaining coins into the purse on his belt and left the house in a hurry.

In the glass factory, the supervisor approached him with a pale face.

"Johan dropped molten glass on his foot and burnt it terribly," he said. "I sent him home. The doctor said he'll not be able to work for at least a month."

Pidder shrugged. All that kept the numbness at bay was the knowledge that he would get money for what his men produced. "Split his hours between the other workers. We need to get more ornaments done fast."

"But, Pidder, they're already working long shifts."

"If they can't work the way I want, I'm sure they'll find work elsewhere." Pidder hurried toward his office. "Make them work harder. I'll make more designs."

"What about Johan?" The supervisor clutched his clipboard to his chest.

"What about him?" Pidder turned at the door.

"You'll need to pay the doctor. And since he can't work for a month due to a work accident, he'll need compensation."

Pidder frowned. "Did I drop the glass on his foot? Get the men to work and stop bothering me with trivia."

$$\circ\ \circ\ \circ$$

During the next few days, Pidder's peddlers returned one by one, each bringing a purse filled to the brim and orders for more ornaments. Pidder hired two more glassblowers and worked overtime to create more designs for the fragile decorations. Soon his peddlers were on their way again. Every night he double-checked the contents of his wooden box. He had bought a sturdy lock and wore the key around his neck. He barely had time for his wife and when he did, he chided her for spending too much money. After a week of near silence, his mother sat down beside him after a dinner of thin potato soup.

"Did you notice how unhappy Lisbeth is? She's working as hard as she can in the garden so we've got enough to eat, although there's no reason for her to do so." She put her hand on her son's arm. "I've seen you count your money at night when I couldn't sleep. It's enough to provide the whole village with a comfortable life. Why not make her life easier by buying the things we need? Your wife shouldn't grow old early like I did."

Pidder's heart contracted. *She's seen me! And she wants me to give away my hard-earned money. No way!* He cleared his throat. "If you're so concerned about the village's welfare, you might as well go back and live on their generosity. You're no longer welcome in my house."

Ignoring the pale, shocked face of his mother, he pushed his chair backward and left the house. Outside he bumped into Lisbeth, who was just returning with a bag of flour from the only shop in the village.

"The merchant says you'll have to pay our bill soon or he won't let me put our wares on our tab any longer." She smiled, which made the dark rings under her eyes stand out.

Pidder frowned. "Stop buying at his shop then."

Lisbeth's eyes widened. "But we need flour and meat and more. We don't have a farm where we could produce things like that. And I'm all alone. How am I supposed to cope?"

"Waste not want not," he said.

Tears filled her eyes. "You're becoming more and more like my father." She ran past him and slammed the door. That night, he slept in the good room, and it didn't bother him. Neither did the fact that his mother had packed her scarce belongings and returned to her ramshackle hut at the forest's edge.

◑ ◑ ◑

"Did you see that?" Elfin stared at Mikael. "He sent his mother to live in poverty and quarreled with his wife. Something is very, very wrong."

Mikael paled and said,. "We need to stop this experiment now, before something worse happens." He got up and walked toward the door.

"Wait, if you show up like this, Pidder will recognize you immediately." Elfin waved his wand, and Mikael changed. His stature shrank, became stockier. He grew a well-rounded belly and a beard, and his clothes turned into that of an itinerant preacher. Holding out his hands to the side and looking down, he glared at Elfin.

"A preacher, really?"

"It seemed less conspicuous than another merchant."

"Fine. I'll ask for a place to spend the night and see what I can do about removing my machines." Mikael left their cave and set out on the deer trail that'd take him downhill, closer to the village.

"If you need my help just call." Elfin's voice sounded as clear in his head as if he had come along.

One of Pidder's peddlers returned early. He couldn't have been to town and back already. Also, his basket was missing. Had he met someone on the way he sold the ornaments to? The man hobbled along the main street supported by a crutch; he hung his head as he approached the glass factory. It didn't look like he had been successful. Pidder, on his way out for lunch, crossed his arms in front of his chest.

"Why are you back so soon?" he asked.

The man barely held himself upright with his crutch. "In the rain yesterday, the trail became slippery. Before I found shelter, I lost my footing and fell."

"And what happened to my wares?" Pidder's voice sounded as level and detached as he felt.

"As I dangled over the ravine, I had to drop the basket or I would never have been able to climb back up."

"You lost my wares?" Suddenly, it occurred to Pidder that with the loss of his wares, he wouldn't get more money. His blood seemed to boil.

"Either that or my life." The man's voice sounded pleading.

"What do I care for your life? Your loss cost me a fortune. I demand compensation." Pidder's eyes sparked, and fire burned in his veins. *What a glorious feeling.* He should be generous to a man who had managed to make him feel. He'd refrain from ruining him and his family. "You'll pay off the worth of what you lost in ten installments. And I'll deduct the costs for the basket."

He stepped past the man who stared at him wordlessly, wide-eyed and with his mouth hanging open. *He could have thanked me for my generosity,* Pidder thought. Resigned, he felt the numbness return. Well, at least he had felt something for a moment. Every little feeling was better than nothing.

When he entered the kitchen of his house, he found a stranger sitting at his table. It was a preacher, barefoot with ragged clothing but a potbelly. And he was eating his food. Lisbeth stood beside the man and refilled his plate.

The world blurred. The fire he had felt before returned and flooded his body. It raged around his mind. How dare Lisbeth feed a stranger with their hard-earned food? Uttering a strangled cry, he grabbed the poker from its stand beside the hearth and slammed it onto Lisbeth's head. He heard her skull crack. Lisbeth dropped like a stone, and the stranger jumped up, shouting at Pidder. But Pidder's world narrowed to a pinpoint where he heard nothing and only saw the lifeless form of his wife on the ground. Blood pooled around her head, her bonnet sat askew, and her hair had come loose. She looked like an angel with a bloody halo.

I've killed her. The thought pierced his soul and seemed to rip him apart. He felt the strange numbness fighting unsuccessfully against this surge of sorrow and guilt. Sinking to his knees, a strangled cry escaped his throat. His eyes burned but not a single tear fell. *I'm a murderer.* The pinpoint of his life narrowed even more. He couldn't take his eyes from the gash on Lisbeth's head. Splinters of pale bone stuck in the clotting blood. He retched. Then he lost consciousness.

◑ ◑ ◑

When he woke, Lisbeth was gone. Only the pool of dried blood reminded him of where she had been. Strangely enough, this didn't disturb him one bit. He felt calm and detached. It was good that he wouldn't need to dispose of the body. No one needed to know about this. Naturally, he'd have to get rid of what was left of the evidence. He fetched a bucket of water and a piece of cloth and cleaned the floor as best he could. While he scrubbed the floor, he wondered why it was so hard for him to feel anything anymore. Could it be his stone heart? When he had washed away all the blood and left the cloth to dry, he sat in the good room and counted his money. But this time the clinking coins didn't give him the satisfaction he usually felt. He wanted Lisbeth back. He tried to recall the softness of her skin or her lips on his, but the memory seemed strangely anemic. He'd killed her. Now he had to learn to live with that burden. He shrugged and went to bed.

♂ ♂ ♂

"Put her here." Elfin pointed to the wide stone table in the room Mikael had used as a lab. "Is she still breathing?"

"Barely. Can you keep her alive for a little longer?" Mikael laid Lisbeth down.

"Miracles are my job, aren't they?" Elfin's voice didn't sound very convincing.

Mikael kept searching through his tools frantically. He didn't know as much about medicine as a professional doctor, but he knew enough to know that Lisbeth's chances of survival were slim. He found the pincers and the sterile needles and thread. He'd do what he could but there were no guarantees. With flying fingers, he picked bone splinters from Lisbeth's wound while Elfin kept the glowing tip of his wand at her temple. The woman's breathing was shallow but didn't stop. Mikael washed the wound with alcohol as best he could and was relieved to see that none of the splinters had dug into the brain matter, only a cracked rectangle was pressing down. Carefully, he pulled the two pieces of bone out. He'd seen soldiers survive a wound like this. Some of them even retained their humanity.

How could it have come to this? A giant hand squeezed his heart as he cut and bent a small piece of metal into a shape big enough to cover the hole in Lisbeth's skull. If she didn't survive, if she didn't fully recover, he'd be at fault. Why had he meddled with Pidder's feelings? He washed the plate and his smallest screws with alcohol thoroughly and then fastened the metal plate onto the skull bone. After washing the wound once more, he pulled the skin over it and sewed it together with his sterile needle and thread. It was all he could do. Now it was up to Elfin to provide a miracle.

The weeks went by and Pidder tried to cover up the loss of his wife. He told Ezekiel that he had sent Lisbeth to a health resort, and was slightly surprised that his father in law believed him. After a few days of sitting at his table at work without a single idea for a new design, he stopped going to work. He didn't leave the house any more, cooked crappy meals when the hunger cramps demanded he eat, and counted his wealth. As long as his fingers did not touch the cool metal, no emotion bothered his stony heart. But when he counted the coins, his heart grew heavy and tears rolled over his cheeks. As long as he held his riches, he knew he should be feeling more than this mixture of numbness and sadness. As long as he held contact with the metal that once brought him so much joy, he managed to recall Lisbeth's face, and sometimes, in extremely precious moments, he remembered her loving smile.

The nightmares began three weeks after what he called the Incident. He dreamed that he woke in the middle of the night and Lisbeth drifted through his bedroom. She wore nothing but a white shift, and her head was wrapped in bandages. She never looked at him, and when he tried to take her into his arms, she was as insubstantial as the air around him. Most mornings he woke lying on the floor of his bedroom, shivering from the cold. *What a nuisance*, he thought. After a breakfast of cold, watery porridge, he dressed and sat down to bury his hands in his money again. There, he understood that his nightmares were a form of punishment from whatever was left of his conscience. *I should be devastated*, he thought. *I should kneel at Ezekiel's feet begging for forgiveness. This stone heart killed me as much as it killed Lisbeth. If only I had never agreed to this bargain.* He shrugged, but felt a single tear teeter on the lashes of his right eye. *I will have to tell the truth and face whatever punishment is coming my way.* With sluggish movements, he put away the money and locked the chest. When he left the good room, the outside door opened and his mother entered the kitchen from the other side. She carried a basket with a small loaf of freshly baked dark bread. She smiled at her son.

"I thought you might need something familiar to cheer you up as long as Lisbeth is gone," she said.

Pidder tried a smile but it felt fake on his face. His heart wasn't in it. How could it be, seeing it was made of stone. Obviously, his mother sensed that something was wrong, because she put her basket aside, pulled her son down on a bench beside the big kitchen table, and took his hands.

"You look as if you've seen a ghost," she said. "I've never seen you like this before. Is there anything I can do?"

Pidder decided to tell her the truth. He'd have to start somewhere anyway. "I earned so much money and it pleased me a lot, but whenever I touch it, I find it's not as important as Lisbeth used to be."

"I knew you'd realize that sooner or later." His mother beamed. Her relief showed in that smile. "You need to tell Lisbeth as soon as she comes back."

"She's not coming back." Pidder noticed how flat and unemotional his voice sounded but he didn't care. Nothing mattered as long as the stone in his chest forced him to forget about how things used to feel.

"Not coming back?" His mother sat straighter and her eyebrows rose. "Nonsense. You'll only need to follow her and tell her you've changed."

"But that's exactly the problem. I haven't changed. There's still this stone in my chest." Pidder got up. "Lowland Mike put it there in exchange for the money I used to buy the glass factory. It stops me from feeling anything at all. I even ki…"

Lisbeth walked through the wall between the good room and the kitchen. This time, she looked at him. Her mouth formed the word "murderer."

Pidder saw his mother pale. When she slipped off the bench, unconscious, he was barely able to catch her before she hit her head on the furniture or the floor. Holding her in his arms, he looked at the ghostly figure.

"You know I don't feel remorse," he said. "I want to. I would like to feel desperate enough to throw myself off the next best cliff, but I don't. The stone in my chest prevents it. My mind insists that I should be sorry, Lisbeth. Therefore, I have decided to face my punishment. But it will not change the way I'm not feeling anything." He lowered his head and sighed. "Believe me, I would give my life to get my heart back if only for a moment. I need to feel the pain I have caused and the grief and guilt that should torment me."

A feathery feeling, like the smallest breeze of air, touched his cheek. He looked up. Lisbeth was crying. Longing shone in her eyes. When she was sure she had caught his attention, she pointed up the mountain. He cocked his head. What did she mean by that? Of course, the gorge!

"You want me to jump into the gorge as a punishment?" His words sounded more like a statement than a question.

Lisbeth frowned and shook her head. She was fading away, drawing a picture into the air with both hands. Just as she vanished completely, Pidder realized she had drawn a fir tree. He slapped his forehead. "The Glassmanikin. Of course. I've still got one wish left."

ⵔ ⵔ ⵔ

Elfin yawned and stretched. "My, is that tiring. If he doesn't show up, we might have to find a different way to clear up the mess we made."

"I'm not going to kill anyone if that's what you're suggesting," Mikael said.

How typical of him to misunderstand. Elfin smiled. "I meant something along the lines of wiping their minds."

"Don't you trust your own spells anymore?" Mikael put a bowl with steaming potatoes on the table and sat down. "That ghost you conjured was pure brilliance."

"We still don't know if Pidder understood." Elfin sat down to eat. He spoke with his mouth full. "If he doesn't show up today, you'll have to force him. My magic will not be safe with the technology you put inside of him."

"Have you ever tried to combine the two?" Mikael sounded curious.

Typical, Elfin thought. *Always searching for another interesting project.* "No, and I don't think it's a good idea. I've seen a few people try, and they all failed."

"I heard that the mother of the Bergian queen managed to create a gadget that uses magic and technology." Mikael filled his plate. "So it seems to be possible."

To Elfin, magic and technology seemed to be mutually exclusive. Like the two sides of a lodestone. But there were lots of things you could do with a lodestone, so why not with magic and technology? He considered this. "One would have to be extremely cautious. Maybe if the magic could be woven around the technology somehow in a way that would keep them from touching…" His voice trailed off.

Before Mikael could say something, the voice of Elfin's door-chime spell called out.

"Visitor reciting the correct poem. Visitor reciting the correct poem."

"Thank you," Elfin said to stop the spell from repeating the message endlessly, and grinned. "It seems Pidder found the way back to the Glassmanikin after all. Let's see what we can do to clear up this mess." He got up, stuffed another piece of potato into his mouth and changed into the long-bearded, dwarfish shape of the Glassmanikin before he vanished.

Elfin felt his body stretch impossibly thin. His head throbbed as he passed through the unseen realm. Normally, he tried to avoid this way of traveling, but it was essential to keep up appearances. He didn't want Pidder to think him incompetent. *Although that's just what I was in this case*, he thought. *Mikael too.* He appeared on a big root of the biggest fir tree in the forest, right below Pidder's nose.

"What can I do for you this time?" He tried to sound gruff, pulled a pipe from his pocket and lit it. "I ain't got all day."

"Please, give me back my heart." Kneeling in the dirt, Pidder lowered his head. "It was a mistake to swap it for a stone. I know that my life is horrible now but I cannot feel it due to the stone."

"If you get it back, you'll have to live with what you did to Lisbeth." Elfin wanted to see how the boy would react to that.

"I've done wrong and will have to live with the consequences." Pidder looked up. "But punishment doesn't mean anything if I don't care about it one bit. I need to feel again, even if it means feeling pain all the time."

Elfin scratched his head.

"Well, it's not a wish I can grant," he said with a sigh.

"I had feared as much." Pidder got up and knocked the soil off the knees of his trousers. He spoke without looking at Elfin, and his tone was flat and devoid of emotion. "If you can't do anything for me, can you revive Lisbeth?"

"No magic in this world can bring back the dead." Phrasing it this way wasn't a lie, Elfin was sure.

"Thank you for your honesty." Pidder nodded as if he had expected the answer. He bowed and turned to leave. "Farewell."

"Where are you going to?" Elfin saw his plan slipping away. He didn't fancy clobbering the human and floating him to Mikael's cave. It would take too much power he might need later.

"I will face my punishment. It will not redeem me, but it is the right thing to do."

Well, at least he has learned something, Elfin thought. "You should talk to Lowland Mike about your heart. After all, you sold it to him."

Pidder shot round faster than Elfin had expected, and his voice carried an edge of emotion. "Do you think he can swap it back?"

"You'd have to trick him." Elfin grinned, even though he didn't feel like smiling at all. He'd feel a lot better once this mess was sorted. What had come over him to start a bet like this? Everybody knew that both magic and technology had their uses. Deciding which was better was like determining whether pears or plums were better. Everyone had his own answer. "Lowland Mike is proud of the work he does, so you should be able to get him to do your bidding if you pretend he did something wrong."

"That sounds like good advice. Thank you, Glassmanikin. I will not bother you again." Pidder bowed and walked away. Elfin watched him until he could no longer see him. Then he emptied his pipe and returned to Mikael the same way he had come. Time was of the essence, so he'd have to put up with the discomfort.

Mikael looked up from the scrying bowl that Elfin had left running since they started the experiment. It was low-level magic that fed itself from the energy if found around itself.

"Why didn't you bring him here?" Mikael stood up and stretched.

"First, he's too big to take him the way I used," Elfin said. "Second, all your tools are in your workroom cave. Why spend energy on getting him there if he's entirely willing to walk?"

"In that case, let's hurry to get there before he does." Mikael grabbed his tool belt. Before he could walk to the cave's exit, Elfin changed him into Lowland Mike again. Then, he renewed the stasis spell surrounding Lisbeth. She looked so peaceful, but the wound in her skull was healing much too slowly. Also, her spirit disconnected again and again. It had been difficult to keep it close enough so the body wouldn't die. On the other hand, it had helped Elfin to create a believable ghost. For a moment, he wondered if Pidder would have come even if he hadn't sent the ghost. He shook his head. Pidder had come, so it didn't matter. Elfin hurried after Mikael.

His friend had already lit countless candles all around the cave.

"You can clean the table," he said when Elfin entered. "It needs to be as clean as you can make it."

Elfin used his wand and removed all dirt and organic life from the stone slate. "Anything else?"

"Done already?"

"That's what magic's for, isn't it? These everyday tasks take so little energy, I don't even notice." Elfin hopped on a stool and looked at the big workbench where Mikael laid out his tools.

"In that case, I can disinfect your tools too."

Mikael stepped aside. "Disinfect?"

"Make them squeaky clean so they can't infect Pidder when you use them on him."

Mikael's grin was slightly lopsided. "That'd be great."

Again, Elfin used his wand. "How are we going to help Pidder?"

Before Mikael could answer, a noise in the cave's entrance made Elfin jump off the stool and hide under the table. Pidder entered and bowed to Mikael.

"Good day, sir."

Mikael pretended to be surprised as he looked up. "Well, if it isn't Pidder Munk. What can I do for you, son?"

"You made a mistake with that heart you gave me." The young man sat on the stool Elfin had just left.

You could say that again, the male fairy godmother thought. *We both made huge mistakes with your heart.*

"My work is as close to perfect as I can get it." Mikael played the role well. "What went wrong with the heart I gave you?"

"I can still feel." Pidder's voice suggested he was glaring at Elfin's friend. "In extreme situations, like when I face death, elation courses through my veins. Also, when I touch money my heart beats faster. I'm sure that's not what this heart should let me feel, seeing it's supposedly made of stone."

"That is strange behavior indeed for a stone heart." Mikael touched Pidder's chest with the index finger of his left hand and pretended to listen. "I'll have to look at it more closely to see what went wrong."

Pidder laughed, but it sounded forced. "I'm sure you never took out my real heart after all."

Touché, Elfin thought. *However, if he really had swapped your heart for a stone, you would have been dead before you woke. Mikael's a genius when it comes to mechanics but hasn't got a drop of magic in his veins.*

"That's where you're wrong." Elfin admired how well Mikael played his role. His deep voice even sounded angry. "I did take it out."

"I am absolutely sure you didn't. After all, I can still feel." Pidder's feet and legs trembled, but only Elfin saw them. "You won't convince me otherwise unless I feel different with my old heart in my chest."

"I will get to that right away." Mikael stepped close enough that Elfin had to withdraw his fingers. "You'll see that you'll feel a lot more with your old heart. When you wake, you'll beg me to return the stone. See, I know what you did, Pidder."

"I already feel things I do not want to feel. So you'd better prove to me that this is not my heart."

Mikael led Pidder to the stone slab table. "If you'd lie down here, I can have a look."

Elfin decided the time had come to anesthetize Pidder. The young man slumped at the flick of his wand, and Mikael caught him before he hit the floor.

"I thought you'd never get to it," he grumbled. Carefully, he laid Pidder on the table and began to undress him. "I'm sure I can remove the filter at his heart with your help. But I'm extremely worried about the one in his brain. It's the one that filters most of the excess emotions. It probably will not be enough to take out the heart's filter."

"Let's take one step at a time." Elfin climbed onto the table. "Am I right in assuming that we've got to open the chest?"

"It'd make things a lot easier if I could get at the gadget directly. The tool I used for placing it would need a lot of adjusting if I wanted to use it for removing it. Also, if there's more bleeding than I anticipate, it'd be best if you could close the wounds immediately. Can you do that?"

Elfin nodded. It would tax his magical strength to keep the torso open for any length of time, but he knew he could do it as long as nothing unexpected happened.

"He might wake up with a scar though," he said.

"Can't be helped." Mikael picked up a very sharp knife. "Let's get started."

A few minutes later, Elfin felt close to puking. The inside of a human wasn't nearly as neat as the outside. And all the blood made him queasy. He swallowed again and again, trying to ignore Mikael's red-stained hands fumbling with the gadget. Instead he concentrated on keeping Pidder breathing. It just wouldn't do to let him die when they were trying to save him from their folly. But the human body drained his magic. Beads of sweat grew on his forehead and his tunic was soaked. His breathing became as labored as that of their patient.

"I've nearly got it," Mikael said. "I've already retracted the retaining brackets. Just one second."

He pulled out a shiny object that looked like a metal spider and dropped it on the floor. "I'll sew him up. Hold on, Elfin."

The fairy godmother saw the concern in Mikael's eyes but couldn't answer. He was too busy keeping the blood from flowing out of Pidder's body, keeping his heart and lungs moving, and keeping him asleep though the ordeal. His field of vision narrowed.

"Hurry up." He breathed the words. A few moments later, he heard what he needed to hear.

"I'm done." Mikael stepped back and wiped the blood off his hands. "Time for a break."

Elfin prodded Pidder's natural resources into healing himself. It'd take a while and he'd have to add a generous amount of magic for it to happen fast, but at least he wasn't working against nature this time. He'd have time to recover. With a sigh, he crumpled.

When he came to, he was lying on Mikael's lap like a small child. His friend looked scared and worried.

"Are you feeling better?"

Elfin nodded and sat up. His stomach grumbled. The magic had used a lot of his energy. "Do we have something to eat?"

Mikael sat Elfin on a cushioned chair and ran off. A few minutes later, he returned with sweetened tea, a piece of cake, and an apple. While Elfin ate, they brainstormed how to remove the filter from Pidder's brain.

"We can't open the skull," Elfin said. "That'd cost even more magic and I'm afraid I won't be able to keep that up for more than a few minutes."

"I don't think I can get it out anyway," Mikael said. "It's attached to the place where most emotions stem from, and that's deep inside the brain. If I try to get in there, either by opening his head or with my tube, I'll destroy parts of his brain tissue. I don't think that would be very good."

"Does that mean we have to leave it in his head?" Elfin drained his cup.

"I'm afraid so."

"But doesn't that mean he'll still be without much emotion?" Elfin wiped his mouth. "I thought you'd said that the brain gadget does most of the filtering and the one near the heart was only a backup in case the first gadget couldn't cope."

Mikael stared at his hands without answering.

"Is there a way you can at least get the filter out of the gadget?" Elfin struggled to keep up hope. As long as they were able to think, they would find a way to help Pidder.

Mikael shrugged. "There are three filters. If they were smaller, they'd probably flush out with a sudden surge of emotions. But they won't shrink by themselves."

"I can try shrinking them." Elated by the new hope, Elfin jumped to his feet. Dizziness forced him to sit down again.

"I thought you can't affect technical gadgets." Mikael looked at him, and his face mirrored Elfin's hope.

"I can't. But I can manipulate individual parts if I know where my magic needs to go and which areas to avoid." Elfin leaned back into the chair. "Recently I've been thinking about this a lot. In my opinion, it should be possible to combine magic and technology if the two forces are kept apart. You see, I can easily affect a table or a horse cart. I should be able to manipulate a lever or a few cogs with my powers. Magic is a delicate power that needs to be balanced well. I think the problems between technology and magic are caused by magical interferences when the power encounters a complex gadget."

Mikael stayed silent and seemed to ponder the idea. After a while, he bent down and picked up the tiny machine he'd removed from Pidder's heart. It still had blood sticking to it. "So, you're trying to say that if I show you exactly how this works, you could probably shrink the filters in the remaining gadget?"

"That's my hope."

The two friends stared at each other for a long time. Finally, Mikael sighed. "Well then, let's take this apart while you recover."

When Pidder woke, he didn't know how much time had passed. Lowland Mike sat on a chair beside the stone table, snoring gently. He didn't look dangerous any more. Still, Pidder thought it better to leave before he woke. When he sat up, his chest hurt. He opened his tunic. A big scar ran from his throat down over his chest. *Woa!* Pidder realized that his chest must have been open. A flutter of concern touched his heart and vanished. *I'm feeling something again*, he thought. *Not as much as I'd like to feel but I do feel something.* Silently, Pidder slipped off the table. His legs buckled, and it took him a while until he managed to stand. Holding on to the table, he began to walk. Soon he had to let go of his support. Wobbly, he reached the wall and steadied himself against it. *How can I be so weak? Changing my heart back seems to have taken a much bigger toll than giving it away.* With trembling legs, he followed the tunnel out of the cave. When he reached daylight, he sighed with relief. The sun was just rising behind the horizon, and he wondered again how long he'd been unconscious. When he took a step toward the forest, his legs protested. They'd need rest soon. Pidder decided to hide in a place where Lowland Mike wouldn't find him and where he could sleep for a while. *Mother will be waiting for me.* The thought popped into his head unbidden. *She will be worried.*

Pain flared through his chest and head, and he doubled over, sinking to his knees. The world around him began to swim. *Mother ... Lisbeth ... oh god, what have I done?* Pidder clutched the shirt over his chest as wave after wave of sorrow, guilt, and fear rippled through him. *How can I ever face this world again knowing what I did to Lisbeth? If only I knew where her body is, I could at least organize a funeral. Hopefully they'll hang me for the murder. Oh, my poor, old mother. It'll break her heart.* Tears spilled from Pidder's eyes, ran over his face, and soaked his tunic. For a fleeting moment he wished his heart was still made of stone before he embraced his feelings. It was better this way, and as soon as he found the strength to walk, he'd visit Ezekiel and tell him what he'd done to his daughter. The rest would not be in his hands any more. He'd be able to bear the consequences as long as he could remember Lisbeth's love. Staggering to his feet, he began the long, tiring walk home.

Mikael stood at the cave's exit and watched the hunched figure walk away.

"It seems to have worked," he said to Elfin. He felt as if a heavy stone had been lifted off his heart.

The fairy godmother stood on a stone beside him, watching Pidder too. "Do you think I should send him the ghost again, just to be on the safe side?"

"First, let's watch him for a while." Mikael started walking uphill toward their living cave. "It'll give us time to decide on how to proceed."

"I wish this was over already. I'm getting really tired of this." Elfin hovered beside him.

"It'll teach us not to meddle like that again." Mikael smiled at his friend.

"It'll teach us to never offer a bet." Elfin grinned. "And now, I need some more food. Will you cook?"

When Pidder arrived at his house, the sun was already setting again. His mother was waiting for him in front of the house. She looked cold and miserable but when she saw him, she ran to embrace him.

"Where have you been this long? I was worried sick." She kissed his face. "I've been waiting for two days and feared the worst."

Wordlessly, Pidder hugged her. Again, tears sprang from his eyes. He was so tired, he could barely stand. His bed. It was calling for him. But first, he'd have to talk to Ezekiel. That was a task that couldn't wait. If his father-in-law decided he should spend the night in jail, he would do so gladly. "Lisbeth…" he whispered.

"What about her?" His mother helped him into the kitchen. "Ezekiel just got a letter from her today. She's enjoying her stay in the capital despite her homesickness and sends her love."

Lisbeth wrote a letter? But that was impossible. He'd killed her. He was absolutely sure about that. How could a dead person write a letter? Maybe it was that preacher. Surely he took her body along. But what game was he playing, and why? If he thought to blackmail Pidder, he was going about it in an extremely strange way.

"Come on, you look horrible. Let's get something hot into you, and then you'd best go to bed." His mother dragged him to the kitchen table and pushed him into a chair before she turned to fire up the hearth.

Pidder thought he could see a small patch of dried blood on the ground between the table and the hearth, but then realized that that would be impossible. He'd scrubbed the floor too thoroughly. His heart clenched and he cried until he had no tears left. What would he do without Lisbeth? It'd be best if the court issued a death sentence.

"I murdered Lisbeth," he whispered.

"Nonsense." His mother put a plate and a mug of steaming coffee in front of him and sat down too. "She wrote a letter, remember?"

"That couldn't have been from her. She's dead." Pidder looked at his mother. She looked even more haggard than he remembered. "And I mistreated you, too. Now that I'm reasonably well off, you shouldn't live in that hut any longer. Will you stay with me until they come to arrest me?"

"Of course I will stay with you if you want me to." His mother smiled. "I'm glad you changed back to the boy I raised."

"I'm still a murderer." Pidder's eyes burned but he couldn't cry any more.

"Why do you keep saying that? What happened to you?"

"It all started when I set out to meet the Glassmanikin." Pidder told her everything—even the parts he didn't really want to share—including Lisbeth's murder and the disappearance of her body. He even showed her his scar. "When I woke, I had my old heart back. At first it felt a little weak, but it's getting better every minute," he concluded his tale. "I am glad I can feel the remorse and guilt again, because it means I'll also remember my love for Lisbeth and the good times we had. I'll need that when I'm in jail."

For a while, his mother stayed silent. A jolt shot through Pidder at the sound of her voice when she spoke again.

"Maybe the preacher took Lisbeth to a hospital, and she wrote the letter because she survived."

A surge of hope filled his heart, driving away his tiredness. If only that was true … It couldn't be. He'd seen the wound … and the blood … No one could survive the transport to the capital, a three day walk, with such a severe injury. It wasn't possible. But what if? What if the preacher had been a warlock or wizard who could take her there faster? Hope filled his heart to the brim. He thought it might burst.

"Before you talk to Ezekiel or the authorities, let us go into town after the weekend to see if we can find her," his mother suggested.

"We will." Energized, he got up. "But right now, I've still got a few things to do." He practically ran into his good room and opened the wooden box with his treasure. Relieved, he noticed that the coins meant nothing to him anymore. Sure, they were useful for living but they held no power over his heart any longer. He stuffed his pockets with silver coins. When he turned, he saw his mother's pale face and her wide open mouth. Hurriedly, he helped her to a chair.

"Pidder! I didn't know you were rich." Her words were barely more than a stunned whisper.

"The money is ill gained. I will do better in the future if I'm allowed to." He handed her the key. "When I have to atone for my crimes, I want you to use the money to make life in the village better for everyone. Maybe it'll be enough to build a school."

"Oh, Pidder." His mother pressed the key to her bony chest. Her eyes filled with tears. "I so hope Lisbeth is still alive."

"So do I, even though she'll never be able to forgive me." He smiled. It felt strange, for his heart teetered on a ridge between despair and hope. But he couldn't linger. He had things to do, debts to pay. "I need to go to the factory now. Will you manage?"

She nodded, so he left.

○ ○ ○

"I think the operation was successful," Elfin said. "He's hired a girl from the poorhouse to help his mother, and he's paying her twice what's normal plus free board and room."

"That's a start." Mikael stirred the soup. "What else?"

"He's told the guy who lost his wares that he doesn't have to pay for the lost goods, he increased the pay for the glassblowers and the charcoal burners, he paid for the burnt glassblower's health costs, and changed the per piece payments of his workers to a per hour payment. All in a few hours." Elfin looked toward the kitchen. "That's a fantastic start, I think."

"He's squandering his money again."

"He's helping others by making it possible for them to help themselves. That's pretty clever." Elfin glared at Mikael.

"Dinner's ready." With a grin, Mikael took the pot with soup and carried it to the table. "When do you think it's time to present our surprise?"

"That's not for you to decide." Lisbeth lifted her gaze from the scrying bowl. "I want to see if he truly is the man again I fell in love with."

"You've got to be careful he doesn't get a shock." Mikael filled a bowl for her. "I'm just glad we managed to clear up most of the mess we made."

"Will that teach you not to meddle in a human's life again?" Lisbeth stood up and approached her place at the table.

"It is my job to meddle in humans' lives." Elfin held out his bowl. "Thank you, that's enough." He turned to her. "But I promise I'll never do it without the person's knowledge again."

"I think I'll write him a letter and then watch him for another week." Lisbeth sat down to eat.

Mikael stared at the soup in his bowl. "You know what? In the end, neither of us won. Both magic and technology caused unnecessary problems. Maybe solving problems is what life's all about."

"You might be right." Elfin smiled at his friend. "But did you notice that only the combination of your technology and my magic saved Lisbeth and returned Pidder to more or less normal?"

"Thus, your bet ends with a tie." Lisbeth's laughter rang through the cave.

Bonus Story: The Big, Fat Pancake
based loosely on a German tale similar to "The Gingerbread Man"

"Paul, look! A pancake with feet running down the street. And I thought I'd seen it all. Turn on your camera. This is going to be the life news of the day."

"Wait a sec. I'll heat up the steam engine and put in a new recording tape."

"Hurry up, you moron or it'll be gone. Do a big headshot first, then we'll cut to the women chasing it and I'll do an interview.

"Ready? Three, two, one … we're life.

"Welcome to KCNP-TV's It's Life!

"I'm your reporter, Peter Dandelion. Today, we're life in Little Uperton, the home of the famous Puss in Boots, and again it is the center of a most interesting sight.

"Paul, show us, please – Thanks.

"We're now in the company of the three lovely ladies who made the living pancake. Can you please tell us how that miracle came to be?"

"Well, Ethel beat some eggs and talked to the batter."

"What Ruth is trying to say is that we were hungry what with Midwinter so near and all…"

"Don't listen to Annie and Ruth. All I did was sing a seasonal song while preparing the batter. And when Ruth put it in our biggest frying pan, it just grew legs. It even turned itself. When it was nicely done from both sides, it jumped out of the pan and ran."

"Why, do you think, it didn't stay to be eaten?"

"I wouldn't know."

"Thank you very much, dear ladies. We will now try to catch up with our hero, the pancake. Tune in again when it's Peter Dandelion calling – cut, over and out.

"It went down the hill toward the forest. Hurry, Paul. There … it … just … passed … the rabit … and the goat … let's see if … we … can … get the … horse to talk.

"Phooo, that pancake is fast.

"This is Peter Dandelion … life … from Little … Uperton. The now famous running pancake managed to escape a hungry hare, a greedy goat and a stout stallion. Please, sir, a word."

"Wchath dcho chou want?"

"Why didn't you eat the pancake?"

"Chchchchrrr. I tchried to, but it chran away."

"Thank you very much, sir. We will now try to catch up with the pancake again. Tune in again when Peter Dandelion is calling – cut, over and out.

"Man, I'm so out of breath, I can't run much longer.

"What do you say, Paul?"

"Let's get ahead of it."

"Hey, that's a great idea. Where is it now anyway?"

"It passed the pigsty and …"

"I see it. It's doubling back. Maybe afraid of the wolf. Let's ambush it here. You take a good shot of it, and I'll jump on it and hold it down.

"Three, two, one, action … This is Peter Dandelion again. I'm now going to jump the pancake for an interview.

"Whoa! Please, sir pancake, stop for a second. I'm Peter Dandelion and I'd like to interview you."

"Interview? You're carrying an oven and I'm already done to perfection."

"That's not an oven. It's a steam-driven camera. The man working it is my camera man Paul Butterboom. Please, sir, stop, or I'll fall off of you and hurt myself."

"Well, OK then. But the minute you're trying to eat me, I'll be gone again."

"Why are you so determined that no one should eat you."

"I am perfect. I need the perfect eater too."

"And what would be a perfect eater for you?"

"Someone who will savor me. Someone who will remember me for the rest of his life. Someone who will be able to understand my perfectness."

"So, you're looking for a gourmet?"

"Gosh, the smell ... I just can't stand it any longer."

"Paul, no!"

"You won't get me ..."

"Now see what you did, Paul! Hurry. Let's at least try to find out whether he'll find his perfect eater. This is Peter Dandelion.

"Where did he go?"

"Back to the village. I'm sorry, Peter."

"No problem. Let's see if we can catch up with him again. Is the camera still running?"

"Yes."

"OK, let's go.

This is Peter Dandelion pursuing the runaway pancake. It is nearing the village but it's a lot slower than before. Paul and I are gaining on it. There. It stops. Maybe another encounter with a hungry stomach. I wonder what it will be this time."

"It's kids, Peter. Three if I'm not mistaken."

"You're right, Paul. And they're standing in front of the local orphanage. They've probably never seen a delicacy like the pancake in their whole lives. Their eyes are sad, their bodies skinny with scraped knees and torn clothing.

But what's that? The little girl touched the pancake. Let's listen in…"

"… are you?"

"I am a perfect pancake."

"You smell delicious. I've never smelled anything like you before. Did you, Tom, Justin?"

"For those of you who can't see, the two younger boys are shaking their heads."

"Where are you running to?"

"I'm looking for the perfect eater."

"If you see him, can you ask him if he's got a little bit to eat for us as well? We only had a slice of bread between the three of us this morning."

"Why's that?"

"No one pays for orphans, and we're not old enough to earn our share yet."

"Have you ever eaten a pancake?"

"We're not eating someone who talks and runs around."

"Would you promise to remember me for the rest of your lives if I allowed you to eat me?"

"As I said, we're not eating a living being."

"But I'm not living. I'm just magical. Once my magic wears off, and that's going to happen pretty soon, I'm nothing but a big, fat pancake. And I taste delicious."

"You want us to eat you?"

"Yes, plea… plea… pl… ease."

"He's tumbling. The girl catches him, but it seems his magic is close to being spent."

"I'll … be … happy … if … you … remember … me … when … you … finish … eating … me."

"We will. I promise."

"Thank y…"

"That's it. The magic is gone. What are the kids waiting for?

Ah, they obviously wanted to make sure that he's not alive any more. Now, they're eating and you can see the delight in their faces. I'm quite sure they'll remember their first ever pancake for the rest of their lives.

This was Peter Dandelion for KCNP-TV's It's Life! Tune in again for next weeks episode – cut and out.

Phoo. That was quite a chase. You know what, Paul? Next week, we'll look into some orphanages. It really is a shame that parentless children aren't treated better than what we've seen today. After all, children are the future of our country. One of them might be the next Metalurgican!"

"Great idea, Peter. But better talk it through with the producer."

"Right. Now, let's see if the kids will sell a slice of that pancake to two hungry reporters."

THE ORIGINAL: THE COLD HEART
by Wilhelm Hauff

Those who travel through Swabia should always remember to cast a passing glance into the Black Forest, not so much for the sake of the trees (though pines are not found everywhere in such prodigious numbers, nor of such a surpassing height), as for the sake of the people, who show a marked difference from all others in the neighborhood around. They are taller than ordinary men, broad-shouldered, have strong limbs, and it seems as if the bracing air which blows through the pines in the morning, has allowed them, from their youth upwards, to breathe more freely, and has given them a clearer eye and a firmer, though ruder, mind than the inhabitants of the valleys and plains. The strong contrast they form to the people living without the limits of the "Wald," consists, not merely in their bearing and stature, but also in their manners and costume. Those of the Schwarzwald of the Baden territory dress most handsomely; the men allow their beards to grow about the chin just as nature gives it; and their black jackets, wide trousers, which are plaited in small folds, red stockings, and painted hats surrounded by a broad brim, give them a strange, but somewhat grave and noble appearance. Their usual occupations are the manufacturing of glass, and the so-called Dutch clocks, which they carry about for sale over half the globe.

Another part of the same race lives on the other side of the Schwarzwald; but their occupations have made them contract manners and customs quite different from those of the glass manufacturers. Their Wald supplies their trade; felling and fashioning their pines, they float them through the Nagold-river into the Neckar, from thence down the Rhine as far as Holland; and near the sea the Schwarzwalder and their long rafts are well known. Stopping at every town which is situated along the river, they wait proudly for purchasers of their beams and planks; but the strongest and longest beams they sell at a high price to Mynheers, who build ships of them. Their trade has accustomed them to a rude and roving life, their pleasure consisting in drifting down the stream on their timber, their sorrow in wandering back again along the shore. Hence the difference in their costume from that of the glass manufacturers. They wear jackets of a dark linen cloth, braces a hand's breadth wide, displayed over the chest, and trousers of black leather, from the pocket of which a brass rule sticks out as a badge of honor; but their pride and joy are their boots, which are probably the largest that are worn in any part of the world, for they may be drawn two spans above the knee, and the raftsmen may walk about in water at three feet depth without getting their feet wet.

It is but a short time ago that the belief in hobgoblins of the wood prevailed among the inhabitants, this foolish superstition having been eradicated only in modern times. But the singularity about these hobgoblins who are said to haunt the Schwarzwald, is, that they also wear the different costumes of the people. Thus it is affirmed of the glass-manikin, a kind little sprite three feet and a half high, that he never shows himself except in a painted little hat with a broad brim, a doublet, white trousers, and red stockings; while Dutch Michel, who haunts the other side of the forest, is said to be a gigantic, broad-shouldered fellow wearing the dress of a raftsman; and many who have seen him say they would not like to pay for the calves whose hides it would require to make one pair of his boots, affirming that, without exaggeration, a man of the middle height may stand in one of them with his head only just peeping out.

The following strange adventure with these spirits is said to have once befallen a young Schwarzwalder:--There lived a widow in the Schwarzwald, whose name was Frau Barbara Munk; her husband had been a charcoal-burner, and after his death she had by degrees prevailed upon her boy, who was now sixteen years old, to follow his father's trade. Young Peter Munk, a sly fellow, submitted to sit the whole week near the smoking stack of wood, because he had seen his father do the same; or, black and sooty and an abomination to the people as he was, to drive to the nearest town and sell his charcoal. Now, a charcoal-burner has much leisure for reflection, about himself and others; and when Peter Munk was sitting by his stack, the dark trees around him, as well as the deep stillness of the forest, disposed his heart to tears, and to an unknown secret longing. Something made him sad, and vexed him, without his knowing exactly what it was. At length, however, he found out the cause of his vexation,--it was his condition. "A black, solitary charcoal-burner," he said to himself; "it is a wretched life. How much more are the glass-manufacturers, and the clock makers regarded; and even the musicians, on a Sunday evening! And when Peter Munk appears washed, clean, and dressed out in his father's best jacket with the silver buttons and bran new red stockings--if then, any one walking behind him, thinks to himself, 'I wonder who that smart fellow is?' admiring, all the time, my stockings and stately gait;--if then, I say, he passes me and looks round, will he not say, 'Why, it is only Peter Munk, the charcoal-burner."

The raftsmen also on the other side of the wood were an object of envy to him. When these giants of the forest came over in their splendid clothes, wearing about their bodies half a hundred weight of silver, either in buckles, buttons or chains, standing with sprawling legs and consequential look to see the dancing, swearing in Dutch, and smoking Cologne clay pipes a yard long, like the most noble Mynheers, then he pictured to himself such a raftsman as the most perfect model of human happiness. But when these fortunate men put their hands into their pocket, pulled out handsful of talers and staked an expensive piece upon the cast of a die, throwing their five or ten florins to and fro, he was almost mad and sneaked sorrowfully home to his hut. Indeed he had seen some of these gentlemen of the timber trade, on many a holy-day evening, lose more than his poor old father had gained in the whole year. There were three of these men, in particular, of whom he knew not which to admire most. The one was a tall stout man with ruddy face, who passed for the richest man in the neighborhood; he was usually called fat "Hesekiel." Twice every year he went with timber to Amsterdam, and had the good luck to sell it so much dearer than the rest that he could return home in a splendid carriage, while they had to walk. The second was the tallest and leanest man in the whole Wald, and was usually called "the tall Schlurker;" it was his extraordinary boldness that excited Munk's envy, for he contradicted people of the first importance, took up more room than four stout men, no matter how crowded the inn might be, setting either both his elbows upon the table, or drawing one of his long legs on the bench; yet, notwithstanding all this, none dared to oppose him, since he had a prodigious quantity of money. The third was a handsome young fellow, who being the best dancer far around, was hence called "the king of the ball-room." Originally poor he had been servant to one of the timber merchants, when all at once he became immensely rich; for which some accounted by saying he had found a pot full of money under an old pine tree, while others asserted that he had fished up in the Rhine, near Bingen town, a packet of gold coins with the spear which these raftsmen sometimes throw at the fish as they go along in the river, that packet being part of the great treasure of the Nibelung, which is sunk there. But however this might be, the fact of his suddenly becoming rich caused him to be looked upon as a prince by young and old.

Often did poor Peter Munk the coal burner think of these three men, when sitting alone in the pine forest. All three indeed had one great fault, which made them hated by every body: this was their insatiable avarice, their heartlessness towards their debtors and towards the poor, for the Schwarzwalder are naturally a kind-hearted people. However, we all know how it is in these matters; though they were hated for their avarice, yet they commanded respect on account of their money, for who but they could throw away talers, as if they could shake them from the pines?

"This will do no longer," said Peter one day to himself, when he felt very melancholy, it being the morrow after a holiday when every body had been at the inn; "if I don't soon thrive I shall make away with myself; Oh that I were as much looked up to and as rich as the stout Hesekiel, or as bold and powerful as the tall Schlurker, or as renowned as the king of the ball-room, and could like him throw talers instead of kreutzers to the musicians! I wonder where the fellow gets his money!" Reflecting upon all the different means by which money may be got, he could please himself with none, till at length he thought of the tales of those people who, in times of old, had become rich through the Dutchman Michel, or the glass-manikin. During his father's lifetime other poor people often made their calls, and then their conversation was generally about rich persons, and the means by which they had come by their riches; in these discourses the glass-manikin frequently played a conspicuous part. Now, if Peter strained his memory a little he could almost recall the short verse which one must repeat near the Tannenbuehl in the heart of the forest, to make the sprite appear. It began as follows:

"Keeper of wealth in the forest of pine, Hundreds of years are surely thine: Thine is the tall pine's dwelling place--"

But he might tax his memory as much as he pleased, he could remember no more of it. He often thought of asking some aged person what the whole verse was. However, a certain fear of betraying his thoughts kept him back, and moreover he concluded that the legend of the glass-manikin could not be very generally known, and that but few were acquainted with the incantation, since there were not many rich persons in the Wald;--if it were generally known, why had not his father, and other poor people, tried their luck? At length, however, he one day got his mother to talk about the manikin, and she told him what he knew already, as she herself remembered only the first line of the verse, but she added, that the sprite would show himself only to those who had been born on a Sunday, between eleven and two o'clock. He was, she said, quite fit for evoking him, as he was born at twelve o'clock at noon; if he but knew the verse.

When Peter Munk heard this he was almost beside himself with joy and desire to try the adventure. It appeared to him enough to know part of the verse, and to be born on a Sunday, for the glass-manikin to show himself. Consequently when he one day had sold his coals, he did not light a new stack, but put on his father's holiday jacket, his new red stockings, and best hat, took his blackthorn stick, five feet long into his hand, and bade farewell to his mother, saying, "I must go to the magistrate in the town, for we shall soon have to draw lots who is to be soldier, and therefore I wish to impress once more upon him that you are a widow, and I am your only son." His mother praised his resolution; but he started for the Tannenbuehl. This lies on the highest point of the Schwarzwald, and not a village or even a hut was found, at that time, for two leagues around, for the superstitious people believed it was haunted; they were even very unwilling to fell timber in that part, though the pines were tall and excellent, for often the axes of the wood-cutters had flown off the handle into their feet, or the trees falling suddenly, had knocked the men down, and either injured or even killed them; moreover, they could have used the finest trees from there only for fuel, since the raftsmen never would take a trunk from the Tannenbuehl as part of a raft, there being a tradition that both men and timber would come to harm, if they had a tree from that spot on the water. Hence the trees there grew so dense and high that is was almost night at noon. When Peter Munk approached the place, he felt quite awe-stricken, hearing neither voice nor footstep except his own; no ax resounded, and even the birds seemed to shun the darkness amidst the pines.

Peter Munk had now reached the highest point of the Tannenbuehl, and stood before a pine of enormous girth, for which a Dutch ship-builder would have given many hundred florins on the spot. "Here," said he, "the treasure-keeper, the glass-manikin no doubt lives," and pulling off his large hat, he made a low bow before the tree, cleared his throat, and said, with a trembling voice, "I wish you a good evening, Mr. Schatzhauser." But receiving no answer, and all around remaining silent as before, he thought it would probably be better to say the verse, and therefore murmured it forth. On repeating the words, he saw, to his great astonishment, a singular and very small figure peep forth from behind the tree. It seemed to him as if he had beheld the glass-manikin, just as he was described, the little black jacket, red stockings, hat, all even to the pale, but fine shrewd countenance of which the people so much talked, he thought he had seen. But alas, as quickly as it had peeped forth, as quickly it had disappeared again. "Mr. Glass-manikin," cried Peter Munk, after a short hesitation, "pray don't make a fool of me; if you fancy that I have not seen you, you are vastly mistaken, I saw you very well peeping forth from behind the tree." Still no answer, only at times he fancied he heard a low, hoarse tittering behind the tree. At length his impatience conquered this fear, which had still restrained him, and he cried, "Wait, you little rascal, I will have you yet." At the same time he jumped behind the tree, but there was no Schatzhauser, and only a pretty little squirrel was running up the tree.

Peter Munk shook his head; he saw he had succeeded to a certain degree in the incantation, and that he perhaps only wanted one more rhyme to the verse to evoke the glass-manikin; he tried over and over again, but could not think of any thing. The squirrel showed itself on the lowest branches of the tree, and seemed to encourage or perhaps to mock him. It trimmed itself, it rolled its pretty tail, and looked at him with its cunning eyes. At length he was almost afraid of being alone with this animal; for sometimes it seemed to have a man's head, and to wear a three cornered hat, sometimes to be quite like another squirrel, with the exception only of having red stockings and black shoes on its hind feet. In short it was a merry little creature, but still Peter felt an awe, fancying that all was not right.

Peter now went away with more rapid strides than he had come. The darkness of the forest seemed to become blacker and blacker; the trees stood closer to each other, and he began to be so terrified that he ran off in a trot, and only became more tranquil when he heard dogs bark at a distance, and soon after descried the smoke of a hut through the trees. But on coming nearer and seeing the dress of the people, he found that having taken the contrary direction he had got to the raftsmen instead of the glass-makers. The people living in the hut were wood-cutters, consisting of an aged man with his son who was the owner, and some grown up grand-children. They received Peter Munk, who begged a night's quarter, hospitably enough without asking his name or residence, they gave him cider to drink, and in the evening a large black cock, the best meal in the Schwarzwald, was served up for supper.

After this meal the housewife and her daughters took their distaffs and sat round a large pine torch, which the boys fed with the finest rosin; the host with his guest sat smoking and looking at the women; while the boys were busy carving wooden spoons and forks. The storm was howling and raging through the pines in the forest without, and now and then very heavy blasts were heard, and it was as if whole trees were breaking off and crashing down. The fearless youths were about to run out to witness this terrific and beautiful spectacle, but their grandfather kept them back with a stern look and these words: "I would not advise any of you," cried he, "to go now outside the door; by heavens he never would return, for Michel the Dutchman is building this night a new raft in the forest."

The younger of them looked at him with astonishment, having probably heard before of Michel, but they now begged their grand papa to tell them some interesting story of him. Peter Munk who had heard but confused stories of Michel the Dutchman on the other side of the forest, joined in this request, asking the old man who and where he was. "He is the lord of the forest," was the answer, "and from your not having heard this at your age, it follows that you must be a native of those parts just beyond the Tannenbuehl or perhaps still more distant. But I will tell you all I know, and how the story goes about him. A hundred years ago or thereabouts, there were far and wide no people more upright in their dealings than the Schwarzwalder, at least so my grandfather used to tell me. Now, since there is so much money in the country, the people are dishonest and bad. The young fellows dance and riot on Sundays, and swear to such a degree that it is horrible to hear them; whereas formerly it was quite different, and I have often said and now say, though he should look in through the window, that the Dutchman Michel is the cause of all this depravity. A hundred years ago then there lived a very rich timber merchant who had many servants; he carried his trade far down the Rhine and was very prosperous, being a pious man. One evening a person such as he had never seen came to his door; his dress was like that of the young fellows of the Schwarzwald, but he was full a head taller than any of them, and no one had ever thought there could be such a giant. He asked for work, and the timber-merchant, seeing he was strong, and able to carry great weights, agreed with him about the wages and took him into his service. He found Michel to be a laborer such as he had never yet had; for in felling trees he was equal to three ordinary men, and when six men were pulling at one end of a trunk he would carry the other end alone. After having been employed in felling timber for six months, he came one day before his master, saying, 'I have now been cutting wood long enough here, and should like to see what becomes of my trunks; what say you to letting me go with the rafts for once?' To which his master replied, 'I have no objection, Michel, to your seeing a little of the world; to be sure I want strong men like yourself to fell the timber, and on the river all depends upon skill; but, nevertheless, be it for this time as you wish.'

"Now the float with which Michel was to go, consisted of eight rafts, and in the last there were some of the largest beams. But what then? The evening before starting, the tall Michel brought eight beams to the water, thicker and longer than had ever been seen, and he carried every one of them as easily upon his shoulder as if it had been a rowing pole, so that all were amazed. Where he had felled them, no one knows to this day. The heart of the timber-merchant was leaping with joy when he saw this, calculating what these beams would fetch; but Michel said, 'Well, these are for my traveling on, with those chips I should not be able to get on at all.' His master was going to make him a present of a pair of boots, but throwing them aside, Michel brought out a pair the largest that had ever been seen, and my grandfather assured me they weighed a hundred pounds and were five feet long.

"The float started; and if Michel had before astonished the wood-cutters, he perfectly astonished the raftsmen; for his raft, instead of drifting slowly down the river as they thought it would, by reason of the immense beams, darted on like an arrow, as soon as they came into the Neckar. If the river took a turn, or if they came to any part where they had a difficulty in keeping the middle stream or were in danger of running aground, Michel always jumped into the water, pushing his float either to the right or to the left, so that he glided past without danger. If they came to a part where the river ran straight, Michel often sprang to the foremost raft, and making all put up their poles, fixed his own enormous pole in the sand, and by one push made the float dart along, so that it seemed as if the land, trees, and villages were flying by them. Thus they came in half the time they generally occupied to Cologne on the Rhine, where they formerly used to sell their timber. Here Michel said, 'You are but sorry merchants and know nothing of your advantage. Think you these Colognese want all the timber from the Schwarzwald for themselves? I tell you no, they buy it of you for half its value, and sell it dear to Holland. Let us sell our small beams here, and go to Holland with the large ones; what we get above the ordinary price is our own profit.'

"Thus spoke the subtle Michel, and the others consented; some because they liked to go and see Holland, some for the sake of the money. Only one man was honest, and endeavored to dissuade them from putting the property of their master in jeopardy or cheating him out of the higher price. However they did not listen to him and forgot his words, while Michel forgot them not. So they went down the Rhine with the timber, and Michel, guiding the float soon brought them to Rotterdam. Here they were offered four times as much as at Cologne, and particularly the large beams of Michel fetched a very high sum.

When the Schwarzwalders beheld the money, they were almost beside themselves with joy. Michel divided the money, putting aside one-fourth for their master, and distributing the other three among the men. And now they went into the public houses with sailors and other rabble, squandering their money in drinking and gambling; while the honest fellow who had dissuaded them was sold by Michel to a slave-trader and has never been heard of since. From that time forward Holland was a paradise to the fellows from the Schwarzwald, and the Dutchman Michel their king. For a long time the timber merchants were ignorant of this proceeding, and before people were aware, money, swearing, corrupt manners, drunkenness and gambling were imported from Holland.

"When the thing became known, Michel was nowhere to be found, but he was not dead; for a hundred years he has been haunting the forest, and is said to have helped many in becoming rich at the cost of their souls of course: more I will not say. This much, however, is certain, that to the present day, in boisterous nights, he finds out the finest pines in the Tannenbuehl where people are not to fell wood; and my father has seen him break off one of four feet diameter, as he would break a reed. Such trees he gives to those who turn from the right path and go to him; at midnight they bring their rafts to the water and he goes to Holland with them. If I were lord and king in Holland, I would have him shot with grape, for all the ships that have but a single beam of Michel's, must go to the bottom. Hence it is that we hear of so many shipwrecks; and if it were not so, how could a beautiful, strong ship as large as a church, be sunk. But as often as Michel fells a pine in the forest during a boisterous night, one of his old ones starts from its joints, the water enters, and the ship is lost, men and all. So far goes the legend of the Dutchman Michel; and true it is that all the evil in the Schwarzwald dates from him. Oh! he can make one rich," added the old man mysteriously; "but I would have nothing from him; I would at no price be in the shoes of fat Hesekiel and the long Schlurker. The king of the ballroom, too, is said to have made himself over to him."

The storm had abated during the narrative of the old man; the girls timidly lighted their lamps and retired, while the men put a sackful of leaves upon the bench by the stove as a pillow for Peter Munk, and wished him good night.

Never in his life had Peter such heavy dreams as during this night; sometimes he fancied the dark gigantic Michel was tearing the window open and reaching in with his monstrous long arm a purse full of gold pieces, which jingled clearly and loudly as he shook them; at another time he saw the little friendly glass-manikin riding upon a huge green bottle about the room, and thought he heard again the same hoarse laughter as in the Tannenbuehl; again something hummed into his left ear the following verse:

"In Holland I wot,
There's gold to be got,
Small price for a lot,
Who would have it not?"

Again he heard in his right ear the song of the Schatzhauser in the green forest, and a soft voice whispered to him, "Stupid Coal-Peter, stupid Peter Munk you cannot find a rhyme with 'place,' and yet are born on a Sunday at twelve o'clock precisely. Rhyme, dull Peter, rhyme!"

He groaned, he wearied himself to find a rhyme, but never having made one in his life, his trouble in his dream was fruitless. When he awoke the next morning with the first dawn, his dream seemed strange to him; he sat down at the table with his arms crossed, and meditated upon the whisperings that were still ringing in his ears. He said to himself, "Rhyme, stupid Peter, rhyme," knocking his forehead with his finger, but no rhyme would come. While still sitting in this mood, looking gloomily down before him and thinking of a rhyme with "place," he heard three men passing outside and going into the forest, one of whom was singing,

"I stood upon the brightest place,
I gazed upon the plain,
And then--oh then--I saw that face,
I never saw again."

These words flashed like lightning through Peter's ear and hastily starting up, he rushed out of the house, thinking he was mistaken in what he had heard, ran after the three fellows and seized, suddenly and rudely, the singer by the arm, crying at the same time, "Stop, friend, what was it you rhymed with 'place?' Do me the favor to tell me what you were singing."

"What possesses you, fellow?" replied the Schwarzwalder. "I may sing what I like; let go my arm, or--"

"No, you shall tell me what you were singing," shouted Peter, almost beside himself, clutching him more tightly at the same time. When the other two saw this, they were not long in falling foul upon poor Peter with their large fists, and belaboring him till the pain made him release the third, and he sank exhausted upon his knees. "Now you have your due," said they, laughing, "and mark you, madcap, never again stop people like us upon the highway."

"Woe is me!" replied Peter with a sigh, "I shall certainly recollect it. But now that I have had the blows, you will oblige me by telling me plainly what he was singing." To this they laughed again and mocked him; but the one who had sung repeated the song to him, after which they went away laughing and singing.

"Face," then said the poor belabored Peter as he got up slowly; "will rhyme with 'place,' now glass-manikin, I will have another word with you." He went into the hut, took his hat and long stick, bid farewell to the inmates, and commenced his way back to the Tannenbuehl. Being under the necessity of inventing a verse, he proceeded slowly and thoughtfully on his way; at length, when he was already within the precincts of the Tannenbuehl, and the trees became higher and closer, he found his verse, and for joy cut a caper in the air. All at once he saw coming from behind the trees a gigantic man dressed like a raftsman, who held in his hand a pole as large as the mast of a ship. Peter Munk's knees almost gave way under him, when he saw him slowly striding by his side, thinking he was no other than the Dutchman Michel. Still the terrible figure kept silence, and Peter cast a side glance at him from time to time. He was full a head taller than the biggest man Peter had even seen; his face expressed neither youth nor old age, but was full of furrows and wrinkles; he wore a jacket of linen, and the enormous boots being drawn above his leather breeches, were well known to Peter from hearsay.

"What are you doing in the Tannenbuehl, Peter Munk?" asked the wood king at length, in a deep, roaring voice.

"Good morning, countryman," replied Peter, wishing to show himself undaunted, but trembling violently all the while.

"Peter Munk," replied Michel, casting a piercing, terrible glance at him, "your way does not lie through this grove."

"True, it does not exactly," said Peter; "but being a hot day, I thought it would be cooler here."

"Do not lie, Peter," cried Michel, in a thundering voice, "or I strike you to the ground with this pole; think you I have not seen you begging of the little one?" he added mildly. "Come, come, confess it was a silly trick, and it is well you did not know the verse; for the little fellow is a skinflint, giving but little; and he to whom he gives is never again cheerful in his life. Peter, you are but a poor fool and I pity you in my soul; you, such a brisk handsome fellow, surely could do something better in the world, than make charcoal. While others lavish big talers and ducats, you can scarcely spend a few pence; 'tis a wretched life."

"You are right, it is truly a wretched life."

"Well," continued Michel, "I will not stand upon trifles, you would not be the first honest good fellow whom I have assisted at a pinch. Tell me, how many hundred talers do you want for the present?" shaking the money in his huge pocket, as he said this, so that it jingled just as Peter had heard it in his dream. But Peter's heart felt a kind of painful convulsion at these words, and he was cold and hot alternately; for Michel did not look as if he would give away money out of charity, without asking any thing in return. The old man's mysterious words about rich people occurred to him, and urged by an inexplicable anxiety and fear, he cried "Much obliged to you, sir, but I will have nothing to do with you and know you well," and at the same time he began to run as fast as he could. The wood spirit, however, strode by his side with immense steps, murmuring and threatening "You will yet repent it, Peter, it is written on your forehead and to be read in your eyes that you will not escape me. Do not run so fast, listen only to a single rational word; there is my boundary already." But Peter, hearing this and seeing at a little distance before him a small ditch, hastened the more to pass this boundary, so that Michel was obliged at length to run faster, cursing and threatening while pursuing him. With a desperate leap Peter cleared the ditch, for he saw that the Wood-spirit was raising his pole to dash it upon him; having fortunately reached the other side, he heard the pole shatter to pieces in the air as if against an invisible wall, and a long piece fell down at his feet.

He picked it up in triumph to throw it at the rude Michel; but in an instant he felt the piece of wood move in his hand, and, to his horror, perceived that he held an enormous serpent, which was raising itself up towards his face with its venomous tongue and glistening eyes. He let go his hold, but it had already twisted itself tight round his arm and came still closer to his face with its vibrating head; at this instant, however, an immense black cock rushed down, seized the head of the serpent with its beak, and carried it up in the air. Michel, who had observed all this from the other side of the ditch, howled, cried, and raved when he saw the serpent carried away by one more powerful than himself.

Exhausted and trembling, Peter continued his way; the path became steeper, the country wilder, and soon he found himself before the large pine. He again made a bow to the invisible glass-manikin, as he had done the day before, and said,

"Keeper of wealth in the forest of pine,
Hundreds of years are surely thine,
Thine is the tall pine's dwelling place,
Those born on Sunday see thy face."

"You have not quite hit it," said a delicate fine voice near him, "but as it is you, Peter, I will not be particular." Astonished he looked round, and lo! under a beautiful pine there sat a little old man in a black jacket, red stockings, and a large hat on his head. He had a tiny affable face and a little beard as fine as a spider's web; and strange to see, he was smoking a pipe of blue glass. Nay, Peter observed to his astonishment, on coming nearer, that the clothes, shoes, and hat of the little man were also of colored glass, which was as flexible as if it were still hot, bending like cloth to every motion of the little man.

"You have met the lubber Michel, the Dutchman?" asked the little man, laughing strangely between each word. "He wished to frighten you terribly; but I have got his magic cudgel, which he shall never have again."

"Yes, Mr. Schatzhauser," replied Peter, with a profound bow, "I was terribly frightened. But I suppose the black cock was yourself, and I am much obliged to you for killing the serpent. The object of my visit to you, however, is to ask your advice; I am in very poor circumstances, for charcoal-burning is not a profitable trade; and being still young I should think I might be made something better, seeing so often as I do how other people have thriven in a short time; I need only mention Hezekiel, and the king of the ball-room, who have money like dirt."

"Peter," said the little man, gravely, blowing the smoke of his pipe a long way off, "don't talk to me of these men. What good have they from being apparently happy for a few years here, and the more unhappy for it afterwards? You must not despise your trade; your father and grandfather were honest people, Peter Munk, and they carried on the same trade. Let me not suppose it is love of idleness that brings you to me."

Peter was startled at the gravity of the little man, and blushed. "No, Mr. Schatzhauser," said he; "idleness is the root of every vice, but you cannot blame me, if another condition pleases me better than my own. A charcoal-burner is, in truth, a very mean personage in this world; the glass manufacturer, the raftsmen, and clock-makers, are people much more looked upon."

"Pride will have a fall," answered the little man of the pine wood, rather more kindly. "What a singular race you are, you men! It is but rarely that one is contented with the condition in which he was born and bred, and I would lay a wager that if you were a glass-manufacturer, you would wish to be a timber-merchant, and if you were a timber-merchant you would take a fancy to the ranger's place, or the residence of the bailiff. But no matter for that; if you promise to work hard, I will get you something better to do. It is my practice to grant three wishes to those born on a Sunday, who know how to find me out. The first two are quite free from any condition, the third I may refuse, should it be a foolish one. Now, therefore, Peter, say your wishes; but mind you wish something good and useful."

"Hurrah!" shouted Peter; "you are a capital glass-manikin, and justly do people call you the treasure-keeper, for treasures seem to be plentiful with you. Well then, since I may wish what my heart desires, my first wish is that I may be able to dance better than the king of the ball-room, and to have always as much money in my pocket as fat Hezekiel."

"You fool!" replied the little man, angrily, "what a paltry wish is this, to be able to dance well and to have money for gambling. Are you not ashamed of this silly wish, you blokish Peter? Would you cheat yourself out of good fortune? What good will you and your poor mother reap from your dancing well? What use will money be to you, which according to your wish is only for the public-house, thereto be spent like that of the wretched king of the ball-room? And then you will have nothing for the whole week and starve. Another wish is now left free to you; but have a care to desire something more rational."

Peter scratched himself behind his ears, and said, after some hesitation, "Now I wish the finest and richest glass-factory in the Schwarzwald, with every thing appertaining to it, and money to carry it on."

"Is that all?" asked the little man, with a look of anxiety; "is there nothing else, Peter?"

"Why you might add a horse and chaise."

"Oh, you stupid Peter!" cried the little man, while he flung his glass pipe against a thick pine so that it broke in a hundred pieces. "Horses? a carriage? Sense, I tell you, sense--common sense and judgment you ought to have wished, but not a horse and chaise. Come, come, don't be so sad, we will do all we can to make it turn out for the best, even as it is, for the second wish is on the whole not altogether foolish. A good glass-factory will support its man; but you ought to have wished judgment and sense in addition; a horse and chaise would come as a matter of course."

"But, Mr. Schatzhauser," replied Peter, "I have another wish left, and might very well wish sense, if I am so much in need of it, as you seem to think."

"Say no more about it. You will get involved in many an embarrassment yet, when you will be glad of being at liberty to obtain your third wish. And now proceed on your way home." Drawing a small bag from his pocket, he said: "There are two thousand florins; let that be enough, and don't come again asking for money, for, if you do, I must hang you up to the highest pine. That is the way I have always acted, ever since I have lived in the forest. Three days ago old Winkfritz died, who had a large glass-factory in the lower Wald. Go there to-morrow morning, and make a fair offer for it. Look well to yourself. Be prudent and be industrious; I will come to see you from time to time, and assist you with word and deed, since you have not wished for common sense. But I must repeat it seriously; your first wish was evil. Guard against frequenting the public-house, Peter, no one who did so, ever prospered long." The little man, while thus talking to him, had taken a new pipe, of the most beautiful glass, from his pocket, charged it with dry fir-apples, and stuck it into his little toothless mouth. Then drawing out a large burning-glass, he stepped into the sun and lighted it. When he had done this, he kindly offered his hand to Peter, added a few more words of salutary advice which he might carry on his way, puffed and blew still faster, and finally disappeared in a cloud of smoke, which smelled of genuine Dutch tobacco, and, slowly curling upwards, vanished amidst the tops of the pines.

On his arrival home, Peter found his mother in great anxiety about him, for the good dame thought in reality her son had been drawn among the recruits. He, however, was in great glee and full of hope, and related to her how he had met with a good friend in the forest, who had advanced him money to begin another trade. Although his mother had been living for thirty years in a charcoal-burner's hut, and was as much accustomed to the sight of sooty people, as any miller's wife is to the floury face of her husband; yet, as soon as her Peter showed her a more splendid lot, she was vain enough to despise her former condition, and said: "In truth, as the mother of a man who possesses a glass-manufactory, I shall indeed be something different from neighbor Kate and Betsy, and shall in future sit more consequentially at church among the people of quality." Her son soon came to terms with the heir of the glass manufactory. He kept the workmen he found, and made them work day and night at manufacturing glass. At first he was well enough pleased with his new trade; he was in the habit of walking leisurely into the factory, striding up and down with an air of consequence and with his hands in his pockets, looking now in one corner, now in another, and talking about various things at which his workmen often used to laugh heartily. His chief delight, however, was to see the glass blown, when he would often set to work himself, and form the strangest figures of the soft mass. But he soon took a dislike to the work; first came only for an hour in the day, then only every other day, and finally only once a week, so that his workmen did just what they liked. All this proceeded from his frequenting the public-house. The Sunday after he had come back from the Tannenbuehl he went to the public-house, and who should be jumping there already but the king of the ball-room; fat Hezekiel also was already sitting by a quart pot, playing at dice for crown-pieces. Now Peter quickly put his hand into his pocket to feel whether the glass-manikin had been true to his word, and lo! his pockets were stuffed full of silver and gold. He also felt an itching and twitching in his legs, as if they wished to dance and caper. When the first dance was over, he took his place with his partner at the top next to the "king of the ball-room;" and if the latter jumped three feet high, Peter jumped four; if he made fantastic and graceful steps, Peter twined and twisted his legs in such a manner that all the spectators were utterly amazed with delight and admiration. But when it was rumored in the dancing-room that Peter had bought a glass manufactory, and when people saw that Peter, as often as he passed the musicians, threw a silver coin to them, there was no end of astonishment. Some thought he had found a treasure in the forest, others were of opinion that he had succeeded to some fortune, but all respected him now, and considered him a made man, simply because he had plenty of money. Indeed that very evening he lost twenty florins at play, and yet his pockets jingled and tingled as if there were a hundred talers in them.

When Peter saw how much respected he was, he could no longer contain himself with joy and pride. He threw away handfuls of money and distributed it profusely among the poor, knowing full well as he did how poverty had formerly pinched him. The feats of the king of the ball-room were completely eclipsed by those of the new dancer, and Peter was nicknamed the "emperor of the ball-room." The most daring gamblers did not stake so much as he did on a Sunday, neither did they, however, lose so much; but then, the more he lost, the more he won. This was exactly what he had demanded from the glass-manikin; for he had wished he might always have as much money in his pocket as fat Hezekiel, and it was to this very man he lost his money. If he lost twenty or thirty florins at a stroke, they were immediately replaced in his own pocket, as soon as Hezekiel pocketed them. By degrees he carried his reveling and gambling further than the worst fellows in the Schwarzwald, and he was oftener called "gambling Peter" than "emperor of the ball-room," since he now gambled almost all the week days. In consequence of his imprudence, his glass manufactory gradually fell off. He had manufactured as much as ever could be made, but he had failed to purchase, together with the factory, the secret of disposing of it most profitably. At length it accumulated to such a degree that he did not know what to do with it, and sold it for half-price to itinerant dealers in order to pay his workmen.

Walking homewards one evening from the public house, he could not, in spite of the quantity of wine he had drunk to make himself merry, help thinking with terror and grief of the decline of his fortune. While engaged in these reflections, he all at once perceived some one walking by his side. He looked round, and behold it was the glass-manikin. At the sight of him he fell into a violent passion, protested solemnly, and swore that the little man was the cause of all his misfortune. "What am I now to do with the horse and chaise?" he cried; "of what use is the manufactory and all the glass to me? Even when I was merely a wretched charcoal-burner, I lived more happily, and had no cares. Now I know not when the bailiff may come to value my goods and chattels, and seize all for debt."

"Indeed?" replied the glass-manikin, "indeed? I am then the cause of your being unfortunate. Is that your gratitude for my benefits? Who bade you wish so foolishly? A glass-manufacturer you wished to be, and you did not know where to sell your glass! Did I not tell you to be cautious in what you wished? Common sense, Peter, and prudence, you wanted."

"A fig for your sense and prudence," cried Peter; "I am as shrewd a fellow as any one, and will prove it to you, glass-manikin," seizing him rudely by the collar as he spoke these words, and crying, "have I now got you, Schatzhauser? Now I will tell you my third wish, which you shall grant me. I'll have instantly, on the spot, two hundred thousand hard talers and a house. Woe is me!" he cried, suddenly shaking his hand, for the little man of the wood had changed himself into red-hot glass, and burned in his hand like bright fire. Nothing more was to be seen of him.

For several days his swollen hand reminded him of his ingratitude and folly. Soon, however, he silenced his conscience, saying: "Should they sell my glass, manufactory and all, still fat Hezekiel is certain to me; and as long as he has money on a Sunday, I cannot want."

"Very true, Peter! But, if he has none?" And so it happened one day, and it proved a singular example in arithmetic. For he came one Sunday in his chaise to the inn, and at once all the people popped their heads out of the windows, one saying, "There comes gambling Peter;" a second saying, "Yes, there is the emperor of the ball-room, the wealthy glass-manufacturer;" while a third shook his head, saying, "It is all very well with his wealth, but people talk a great deal about his debts, and somebody in town has said that the bailiff will not wait much longer before he distrains upon him."

At this moment the wealthy Peter saluted the guests at the windows, in a haughty and grave manner, descended from his chaise, and cried: "Good evening, mine Host of the Sun. Is fat Hezekiel here?"

To this question a deep voice answered from within: "Only come in, Peter; your place is kept for you, we are all here, at the cards already."

Peter entering the parlor, immediately put his hand into his pocket, and perceived, by its being quite full, that Hezekiel must be plentifully supplied. He sat down at the table among the others and played, losing and winning alternately; thus they kept playing till night, when all sober people went home. After having continued for some time by candle-light, two of the gamblers said: "Now it is enough, and we must go home to our wives and children."

But Peter challenged Hezekiel to remain. The latter was unwilling, but said, after a while, "Be it as you wish; I will count my money, and then we'll play dice at five florins the stake, for any thing lower is, after all, but child's play." He drew his purse, and, after counting, found he had a hundred florins left; now Peter knew how much he himself had left, without counting first. But if Hezekiel had before won, he now lost stake after stake, and swore most awfully. If he cast identical numbers, Peter immediately cast likewise, and always two points higher. At length he put down the last five florins on the table, saying, "Once more; and if I lose this stake also, yet I will not leave off; you will then lend me some of the money you have won now, Peter; one honest fellow helps the other."

"As much as you like, even if it were a hundred florins," replied Peter, joyful at his gain, and fat Hezekiel rattled the dice and threw up fifteen; "Identical!" he exclaimed, "now we'll see!"

But Peter threw up eighteen, and, at this moment, a hoarse, well-known voice said behind him, "So! that was the last."

He looked round, and behind him stood the gigantic figure of Michel the Dutchman. Terrified, he dropped the money he had already taken up. But fat Hezekiel, not seeing Michel, demanded that Peter should advance him ten florins for playing. As if in a dream Peter hastily put his hand into his pocket, but there was no money; he searched in the other pocket, but in vain; he turned his coat inside out, not a farthing, however, fell out; and at this instant he first recollected his first wish; viz., to have always as much money in his pocket as fat Hezekiel. All had now vanished like smoke.

The host and Hezekiel looked at him with astonishment as he still searched for and could not find his money; they would not believe that he had no more left; but when they at length searched his pockets, without finding any thing, they were enraged, swearing that gambling Peter was an evil wizard, and had wished away all the money he had won home to his own house. Peter defended himself stoutly, but appearances were against him. Hezekiel protested he would tell this shocking story to all the people in the Schwarzwald, and the host vowed he would, the following morning early go into the town and inform against Peter as a sorcerer, adding that he had no doubt of his being burnt alive. Upon this they fell furiously upon him, tore off his coat, and kicked him out of doors.

Not one star was twinkling in the sky to lighten Peter's way as he sneaked sadly towards his home, but still he could distinctly recognize a dark form striding by his side, which at length said, "It is all over with you, Peter Munk; all your splendor is at an end, and this I could have foretold you even at the time when you would not listen to me, but rather ran to the silly glass dwarf. You now see to what you have come by disregarding my advice. But try your fortune with me this time, I have compassion on your fate. No one ever yet repented of applying to me, and if you don't mind the walk to the Tannenbuehl, I shall be there all day to-morrow and you may speak to me, if you will call." Peter now very clearly perceived who was speaking to him, but feeling a sensation of awe, he made no answer and ran towards home.

When, on the Monday morning, he came to his factory, he not only found his workmen, but also other people whom no one likes to see; viz., the bailiff and three beadles. The bailiff wished Peter good morning, asked him how he had slept, and then took from his pocket a long list of Peter's creditors, saying, with a stern look, "Can you pay or not? Be short, for I have no time to lose, and you know it is full three leagues to the prison." Peter in despair confessed he had nothing left, telling the bailiff he might value all the premises, horses, and carts. But while they went about examining and valuing the things, Peter said to himself, "Well, it is but a short way to the Tannenbuehl, and as the little man has not helped me, I will now try for once the big man." He ran towards the Tannenbuehl as fast as if the beadles were at his heels. On passing the spot where the glass-manikin had first spoken to him, he felt as if an invisible hand were stopping him, but he tore himself away and ran onwards till he came to the boundary which he had well marked. Scarcely had he, almost out of breath, called, "Dutch Michel, Mr. Dutch Michel!" than suddenly the gigantic raftsman with his pole stood before him.

"Have you come then?" said the latter, laughing. "Were they going to fleece you and sell you to your creditors? Well, be easy, all your sorrow comes, as I have always said, from the little glass-manikin, the Separatist and Pietist. When one gives, one ought to give right plentifully and not like that skinflint. But come," he continued, turning towards the forest, "follow me to my house, there we'll see whether we can strike a bargain."

"Strike a bargain?" thought Peter. "What can he want of me, what can I sell to him? Am I perhaps to serve him, or what is it that he can want?" They went at first up-hill over a steep forest path, when all at once they stopped at a dark, deep, and almost perpendicular ravine. Michel leaped down as easily as he would go down marble steps; but Peter almost fell into a fit when he saw him below, rising up like a church steeple reaching him an arm as long as a scaffolding pole with a hand at the end as broad as the table in the ale house, and calling in a voice which sounded like the deep tones of a death bell, "Set yourself boldly on my hand, hold fast by the fingers and you will not fall off." Peter, trembling, did as he was ordered, sat down upon his hand and held himself fast by the thumb of the giant.

They now went down a long way and very deep, yet, to Peter's astonishment, it did not grow darker; on the contrary, the daylight seemed rather to increase in the chasm, and it was sometime before Peter's eyes could bear it. Michel's stature became smaller as Peter came lower down, and he stood now in his former size before a house just like those of the wealthy peasants of the Schwarzwald. The room into which Peter was led differed in nothing but its appearance of solitariness from those of other people. The wooden clock, the stove of Dutch tiles, the broad benches and utensils on the shelves were the same as anywhere else. Michel told him to sit down at the large table, then went out of the room and returned with a pitcher of wine and glasses. Having filled these, they now began a conversation, and Dutch Michel expatiated on the pleasures of the world, talked of foreign countries, fine cities and rivers, so that Peter, at length, feeling a yearning after such sights, candidly told Michel his wish.

"If you had courage and strength in your body to undertake any thing, could a few palpitations of your stupid heart make you tremble; and the offenses against honor, or misfortunes, why should a rational fellow care, for either? Did you feel it in your head when they but lately called you a cheat and a scoundrel? Or did it give you a pain in your stomach, when the bailiff came to eject you from your house? Tell me, where was it you felt pain?"

"In my heart," replied Peter, putting his hand on his beating breast, for he felt as if his heart was anxiously turning within him.

"Excuse me for saying so, but you have thrown away many hundred florins on vile beggars and other rabble; what has it profited you? They have wished you blessings and health for it; well, have you grown the healthier for that? For half that money you might have kept a physician. A blessing, a fine blessing forsooth, when one is distrained upon and ejected! And what was it that urged you to put your hand into your pocket, as often as a beggar held out his broken hat?--Why your heart again, and ever your heart, neither your eyes, nor your tongue, nor your arms, nor your legs, but your heart; you have, as the proverb truly says, taken too much to heart."

"But how can we accustom ourselves to act otherwise? I take, at this moment, every possible pains to suppress it, and yet my heart palpitates and pains me."

"You, indeed, poor fellow!" cried Michel, laughing; "you can do nothing against it; but give me this scarcely palpitating thing, and you will see how comfortable you will then feel."

"My heart to you?" cried Peter, horrified. "Why, then, I must die on the spot! Never!"

"Yes, if one of your surgeons would operate upon you and take out your heart, you must indeed die; but with me it is a different thing; just come in here and convince yourself."

Rising at these words, he opened the door of a chamber and took Peter in. On stepping over the threshold, his heart contracted convulsively, but he minded it not, for the sight that presented itself was singular and surprising. On several shelves glasses were standing, filled with a transparent liquid, and each contained a heart. All were labeled with names which Peter read with curiosity; there was the heart of the bailiff in F., that of fat Hezekiel, that of the "king of the ball-room," that of the ranger; there were the hearts of six usurious corn-merchants, of eight recruiting officers, of three money-brokers; in short, it was a collection of the most respectable hearts twenty leagues around.

"Look!" said Dutch Michel, "all these have shaken off the anxieties and cares of life; none of these hearts any longer beat anxiously and uneasily, and their former owners feel happy now they have got rid of the troublesome guest."

"But what do they now carry in their breasts instead?" asked Peter, whose head was nearly swimming at what he beheld.

"This," replied he, taking out of a small drawer, and presenting to him--a heart of stone.

"Indeed!" said Peter, who could not prevent a cold shuddering coming over him. "A heart of marble? But, tell me, Mr. Michel, such a heart must be very cold in one's breast."

"True, but very agreeably cool. Why should a heart be warm? For in winter its warmth is of little use, and good strong cherry-schnaps does more than a warm heart, and in summer when all is hot and sultry, you can't think how cooling such a heart is. And, as before said, such a heart feels neither anxiety nor terror, neither foolish compassion nor other grief."

"And that is all you can offer me," asked Peter, indignantly, "I looked for money and you are going to give me a stone."

"Well! an hundred thousand florins, methinks, would suffice you for the present. If you employ it properly, you may soon make it a million."

"An hundred thousand!" exclaimed the poor coal-burner, joyfully. "Well, don't beat so vehemently in my bosom, we shall soon have done with one another. Agreed, Michel, give me the stone, and the money, and the alarum you may take out of its case."

"I always thought you were a reasonable fellow," replied Michel, with a friendly smile; "come, let us drink another glass, and then I will pay you the money."

They went back to the room and sat down again to the wine, drinking one glass after another till Peter fell into a profound sleep.

He was awakened by the cheerful blast of a post-boy's bugle, and found himself sitting in a handsome carriage, driving along on a wide road. On putting his head out he saw in the airy distance the Schwarzwald lying behind him. At first he could scarcely believe that it was his own self sitting in the carriage, for even his clothes were different from those he had worn the day before; but still he had such a distinct recollection that, giving up at length all these reflections, he exclaimed, "I am Peter and no other, that is certain."

He was astonished that he could no longer, in the slightest degree, feel melancholy now he for the first time departed from his quiet home and the forests where he had lived so long. He could not even press a tear out of his eyes or utter a sigh, when he thought of his mother, who must now feel helpless and wretched; for he was indifferent to every thing: "Well," he said, "tears and sighs, yearning for home and sadness proceed indeed from the heart, but thanks to Dutch Michel, mine is of stone and cold." Putting his hand upon his breast, he felt all quiet and no emotion. "If Michel," said he, beginning to search the carriage, "keeps his word as well with respect to the hundred thousand florins as he does with the heart, I shall be very glad." In his search he found articles of dress of every description he could wish, but no money. At length, however, he discovered a pocket containing many thousand talers in gold, and bills on large houses in all the great cities. "Now I have what I want," thought he, squeezed himself into the corner of the carriage and went into the wide world.

For two years he traveled about in the world, looked from his carriage to the right and left up the houses, but whenever he alighted he looked at nothing except the sign of the hotel, and then ran about the town to see the finest curiosities. But nothing gladdened him, no pictures, no building, no music, no dancing, nor any thing else had any interest for, or excited his stone heart; his eyes and ears were blunted for every thing beautiful. No enjoyment was left him but that which he felt in eating and drinking and sleep; and thus he lived running through the world without any object, eating for amusement and sleeping from ennui. From time to time he indeed remembered that he had been more cheerful and happier, when he was poor and obliged to work for a livelihood. Then he was delighted by every beautiful prospect in the valley, by music and song, then he had for hours looked in joyful expectation towards the frugal meal which his mother was to bring him to the kiln.

When thus reflecting on the past, it seemed very strange to him, that now he could not even laugh, while formerly he had laughed at the slightest joke. When others laughed, he only distorted his mouth out of politeness, but his heart did not sympathize with the smile. He felt he was indeed exceedingly tranquil, but yet not contented. It was not a yearning after home, nor was it sadness, but a void, desolate feeling, satiety and a joyless life that at last urged him to his home.

When, after leaving Strasbourg, he beheld the dark forest of his native country; when for the first time he again saw the robust figures, the friendly and open countenances of the Schwarzwalder; when the homely, strong, and deep, but harmonious sounds struck upon his ear, he quickly put his hand upon his heart, for his blood flowed faster, thinking he must rejoice and weep at the same time; but how could he be so foolish? he had a heart of stone, and stones are dead and can neither smile nor weep.

His first walk was to Michel who received him with his former kindness. "Michel," said he, "I have now traveled and seen every thing, but all is dull stuff and I have only found ennui. The stone I carry about with me in my breast, protects me against many things; I never get angry, am never sad, but neither do I ever feel joyful, and it seems as if I was only half alive. Can you not infuse a little more life into my stone heart, or rather, give me back my former heart? During five-and-twenty years I had become quite accustomed to it, and though it sometimes did a foolish thing, yet it was, after all, a merry and cheerful heart."

The sylvan spirit laughed grimly and sarcastically at this, answering, "When once you are dead, Peter Munk, it shall not be withheld; then you shall have back your soft, susceptible heart, and may then feel whatever comes, whether joy or sorrow. But here, on this side of the grave, it can never be yours again. Traveled you have indeed, Peter, but in the way you lived, your traveling could afford you no satisfaction. Settle now somewhere in the world, build a house, marry, and employ your capital; you wanted nothing but occupation; being idle, you felt ennui, and now you lay all the blame to this innocent heart." Peter saw that Michel was right with respect to idleness, and therefore proposed to himself to become richer and richer. Michel gave him another hundred thousand florins, and they parted as good friends.

The report soon spread in Schwarzwald that "Coal Peter," or "gambling Peter" had returned, and was much richer than before. It was here as it always is. When he was a beggar he was kicked out of the inn, but now he had come back wealthy, all shook him by the hand when he entered on the Sunday afternoon, praised his horse, asked about his journey, and when he began playing for hard dollars with fat Hezekiel, he stood as high in their estimation as ever before. He no longer followed the trade of glass manufacturer, but the timber trade, though that only in appearance, his chief business being in corn and money transactions. Half the people of the Schwarzwald became by degrees his debtors, and he lent money only at ten per cent., or sold corn to the poor who, not being able to pay ready money, had to purchase it at three times its value. With the bailiff he now stood on a footing of the closest friendship, and if any one failed paying Mr. Peter Munk on the very day the money was due, the bailiff with his beadles came, valued house and property, sold all instantly, and drove father, mother, and child, out into the forest. This became at first rather troublesome to Peter, for the poor outcasts besieged his doors in troops, the men imploring indulgence, the women trying to move his stony heart, and the children moaning for a piece of bread. But getting a couple of large mastiffs, he soon put an end to this cat's music, as he used to call it, for he whistled and set them on the beggars, who dispersed screaming. But the most troublesome person to him was "the old woman," who, however, was no other than Frau Munk, Peter's mother. She had been reduced to great poverty and distress, when her house and all was sold, and her son, on returning wealthy, had troubled himself no more about her. So she came sometimes before his house, supporting herself on a stick, as she was aged, weak, and infirm; but she no more ventured to go in, as he had on one occasion driven her out; and she was much grieved at being obliged to prolong her existence by the bounties of other people, while her own son might have prepared for her a comfortable old age. But his cold heart never was moved by the sight of the pale face and well known features, by the imploring looks, outstretched withered hands and decaying frame. If on a Saturday she knocked at the door, he put his hand grumbling into his pocket for some silver coins, wrapped them in a bit of paper and sent them out by a servant. He heard her tremulous voice when she thanked him, and wished him a blessing in this world, he heard her crawl away coughing from the door, but he thought of nothing, except that he had again spent silver for nothing.

At length Peter took it into his head to marry. He knew that every father in the Schwarzwald would gladly give him his daughter, but he was fastidious in his choice, for he wished that every body should praise his good fortune and understanding in matrimony as well as in other matters. He therefore rode about the whole forest, looking out in every direction, but none of the pretty Schwarzwalder girls seemed beautiful enough for him. Having finally looked out in vain for the most beautiful at all the dancing-rooms, he was one day told the most beautiful and most virtuous girl in the whole forest was the daughter of a poor wood-cutter. He heard she lived quiet and retired, was industrious and managed her father's household well, and that she was never seen at a dancing-room, not even at Whitsuntide or the Kirchweihfest (A great festival in German villages, general during the months of October and November). When Peter heard of this wonder of the Schwarzwald, he determined to court her, and, having inquired where the hut was, rode there. The father of the beautiful Elizabeth received the great gentleman with astonishment, but was still more amazed when he heard it was the rich Herr Peter who wished to become his son-in-law. Thinking all his cares and poverty would now be at an end, he did not hesitate long in giving his consent, without even asking the beautiful Elizabeth, and the good child was so dutiful that she became Frau Peter Munk without opposition.

But the poor girl did not find the happiness she had dreamt of. She believed she understood the management of a house well, but she could never give satisfaction to Herr Peter; she had compassion on poor people, and, as her husband was wealthy, thought it no sin to give a poor woman a penny, or a dram to a poor aged man. This being one day found out by Peter, he said to her, with angry look and gruff voice, "Why do you waste my property upon ragamuffins and vagabonds? Have you brought any thing of your own to the house that you can give away? With your father's beggar's staff you could not warm a soup, and you lavish my money like a princess. Once more let me find you out, and you shall feel my hand." The beautiful Elizabeth wept in her chamber over the hard heart of her husband, and often wished herself at home in her father's poor hut rather than with the rich, but avaricious and sinful

Peter. Alas! had she known that he had a heart of marble and could neither love her nor any body else, she would not, perhaps, have wondered. But as often as a beggar now passed while she was sitting before the door, and drawing his hat off, asked for alms, she shut her eyes that she might not behold the distress, and closed her hand tight that she might not put it involuntarily in her pocket and take out a kreutzer. This caused a report and obtained an ill name for Elizabeth in the whole forest, and she was said to be even more miserly than Peter Munk. But one day Frau Elizabeth was again sitting before the door spinning and humming an air, for she was cheerful because it was fine weather, and Peter was taking a ride in the country, when a little old man came along the road, carrying a large heavy bag, and she heard him panting at a great distance. Sympathizing, she looked at him and thought how cruel it was to place such a heavy burden upon an aged man.

In the meanwhile the little man came near, tottering and panting, and sank under the weight of his bag almost down on the ground just as he came opposite Frau Elizabeth.

"Oh, have compassion on me, good woman, and give me a drink of water," said the little man, "I can go no farther, and must perish from exhaustion."

"But you ought not to carry such heavy loads at your age?" said she.

"No more I should if I were not obliged to work as carrier from poverty and to prolong my life," replied he. "Ah, such rich ladies as you know not how painful poverty is, and how strengthening a fresh drought in this hot weather."

On hearing this she immediately ran into the house, took a pitcher from the shelf and filled it with water; but she had only gone a few paces back to take it to him, when, seeing the little man sit on his bag miserable and wretched, she felt pity for him, and recollecting that her husband was from home, she put down the pitcher, took a cup, filled it with wine, put a loaf of rye bread on it and gave it to the poor old man. "There," she said, "a drought of wine will do you more good than water, as you are very old; but do not drink so hastily, and eat some bread with it."

The little man looked at her in astonishment till the big tears came into his eyes; he drank and said, "I have grown old, but have seen few people who were so compassionate and knew how to spend their gifts so handsomely and cordially as you do, Frau Elizabeth. But you will be blessed for it on earth; such a heart will not remain unrequited."

"No, and she shall have her reward on the spot," cried a terrible voice, and looking round they found it was Herr Peter with a face as red as scarlet. "Even my choicest wine you waste upon beggars, and give my own cup to the lips of vagabonds? There, take your reward." His wife fell prostrate before him and begged his forgiveness, but the heart of stone knew no pity, and flourishing the whip he held in his hand he struck her with the ebony handle on her beautiful forehead with such vehemence, that she sunk lifeless into the arms of the old man. When he saw what he had done it was almost as if he repented of the deed immediately; he stooped to see whether there was yet life in her, but the little man said in a well-known voice, "Spare your trouble, Peter; she was the most beautiful and lovely flower in the Schwarzwald, but you have crushed it and never again will see it bloom."

Now the blood fled from Peter's cheek and he said, "It is you then, Mr. Schatzhauser? well, what is done is done then, and I suppose this was to happen. But I trust you will not inform against me."

"Wretch," replied the glass-manikin, "what would it profit me if I brought your mortal part to the gallows? It is not earthly tribunals you have to fear, but another and more severe one; for you have sold your soul to the evil one."

"And if I have sold my heart," cried Peter, "it is no one's fault but yours and your deceitful treasures; your malicious spirit brought me to ruin; you forced me to seek help from another, and upon you lies the whole responsibility." He had scarcely uttered these words than the little man grew enormously tall and broad, his eyes it is said became as large as soup plates, and his mouth like a heated furnace vomiting flames. Peter fell upon his knees, and his stone heart did not protect his limbs from trembling like an aspen leaf. The sylvan spirit seized him, as if with vultures' claws, by the nape of the neck, whirled him round as the storm whirls the dry leaves, and dashed him to the ground so that his ribs cracked within him. "You worm of dust," he cried, in a voice roaring like thunder, "I could crush you if I wished, for you have trespassed against the lord of the forest; but for the sake of this dead woman that fed and refreshed me, I give you a week's respite. If you do not repent I shall return and crush your bones, and you will go hence in your sins."

It was already evening when some men passing by saw the wealthy Peter Munk lying on the ground. They turned him over and over to see whether there was still life in him, but for a long time looked in vain. At length one of them went into the house, fetched some water and sprinkled some on his face. Peter fetched a deep sigh and opened his eyes, looked for a long time around, and asked for his wife Elizabeth, but no one had seen her. He thanked the men for their assistance, crawled into his house, searched everywhere, but in vain, and found what he imagined to be a dream a sad reality. As he was now quite alone strange thoughts came into his mind; he did not indeed fear any thing, for his heart was quite cold; but when he thought of the death of his wife his own forcibly came to his mind, and he reflected how laden he should go hence--heavily laden with the tears of the poor; with thousands of the curses of those who could not soften his heart; with the lamentations of the wretched on whom he had set his dogs; with the silent despair of his mother; with the blood of the beautiful and good Elizabeth; and yet he could not even so much as give an account of her to her poor old father, should he come and ask "Where is my daughter, your wife?" How then could he give an account to Him--to Him to whom belong all woods, all lakes, all mountains, and the life of men?

This tormented him in his dreams at night, and he was awoke every moment by a sweet voice crying to him "Peter, get a warmer heart!" And when he was awoke he quickly closed his eyes again, for the voice uttering this warning to him could be none other but that of his Elizabeth. The following day he went into the inn to divert his thoughts, and there met his friend, fat Hezekiel. He sat down by him and they commenced talking on various topics, of the fine weather, of war, of taxes, and lastly, also of death, and how such and such a person had died suddenly. Now Peter asked him what he thought about death, and how it would be after death. Hezekiel replied, "That the body was buried, but that the soul went either up to heaven or down to hell."

"Then the heart also is buried?" asked Peter, anxiously.

"To be sure that also is buried."

"But supposing one has no longer a heart?" continued Peter.

Hezekiel gave him a terrible look at these words. "What do you mean by that? Do you wish to rally me? Think you I have no heart?"

"Oh, heart enough, as firm as stone," replied Peter.

Hezekiel looked in astonishment at him, glancing round at the same time to see whether they were overheard, and then said, "Whence do you know that? Or does your own perhaps no longer beat within your breast?"

"It beats no longer, at least, not in my breast;" replied Peter Munk. "But tell me, as you know what I mean, how will it be with our hearts?"

"Why does that concern you, my good fellow?" answered Hezekiel, laughing. "Why you have plenty here upon earth, and that is sufficient. Indeed, the comfort of our cold hearts is that no fear at such thoughts befalls us."

"Very true, but still one cannot help thinking of it, and though I know no fear now, still I well remember how I was terrified at hell when yet an innocent little boy."

"Well, it will not exactly go well with us," said Hezekiel; "I once asked a schoolmaster about it, who told me that the hearts are weighed after death to ascertain the weight of their sins. The light ones rise, the heavy sink, and methinks our stone hearts will weigh heavy enough."

"Alas, true," replied Peter; "I often feel uncomfortable that my heart is so devoid of sympathy, and so indifferent when I think of such things." So ended their conversation.

But the following night Peter again heard the well-known voice whispering into his ear five or six times, "Peter, get a warmer heart!" He felt no repentance at having killed his wife, but when he told the servants that she had gone on a journey, he always thought within himself, where is she gone to? Six days had thus passed away, and he still heard the voice at night, and still thought of the sylvan spirit and his terrible menace; but on the seventh morning, he jumped up from his couch and cried, "Well, then, I will see whether I can get a warmer heart, for the cold stone in my breast makes my life only tedious and desolate." He quickly put on his best dress, mounted his horse, and rode towards the Tannenbuehl.

Having arrived at that part where the trees stand thickest, he dismounted, and went with a quick pace towards the summit of the hill, and as he stood before the thick pine he repeated the following verse:

"Keeper of wealth in the forest of pine,
Hundreds of years are surely thine:
Thine is the tall pine's dwelling place--

Those born on Sunday see thy face."

The glass-manikin appeared, not looking friendly and kindly as formerly, but gloomy and sad; he wore a little coat of black glass, and a long glass crape hung floating from his hat, and Peter well knew for whom he mourned.

"What do you want with me, Peter Munk?" asked he with a stern voice.

"I have one more wish, Mr. Schatzhauser," replied Peter, with his look cast down.

"Can hearts of stone still wish?" said the former. "You have all your corrupt mind can need, and I could scarcely fulfill your wish."

"But you have promised to grant me three wishes, and one I have still left."

"I can refuse it if it is foolish," continued the spirit; "but come, let me hear what you wish."

"Well, take the dead stone out of me, and give me a living heart," said Peter.

"Have I made the bargain about the heart with you?" asked the glass-manikin. "Am I the Dutch Michel, who gives wealth and cold hearts? It is of him you must seek to regain your heart."

"Alas! he will never give it back," said Peter.

"Bad as you are, yet I feel pity for you," continued the little man, after some consideration; "and as your wish is not foolish, I cannot at least refuse my help. Hear then. You can never recover your heart by force, only by stratagem, but probably you will find it without difficulty; for Michel will ever be stupid Michel, although he fancies himself very shrewd. Go straightway to him, and do as I tell you." He now instructed Peter fully, and gave him a small cross of pure glass, saying, "He cannot touch your life and will let you go when you hold this before him and repeat a prayer. When you have obtained your wish return to me."

112

Peter took the cross, impressed all his words on his memory, and started on his way to the Dutchman Michel's residence; there he called his name three times and immediately the giant stood before him.

"You have slain your wife?" he asked, with a grim laugh. "I should have done the same, she wasted your property on beggars; but you will be obliged to leave the country for some time; and I suppose you want money and have come to get it?"

"You have hit it," replied Peter; "and pray let it be a large sum, for it is a long way to America."

Michel leading the way they went into his cottage; there he opened a chest containing much money and took out whole rolls of gold. While he was counting it on the table Peter said, "You're a wag, Michel. You have told me a fib, saying that I had a stone in my breast, and that you had my heart."

"And is it not so then?" asked Michel, astonished. "Do you feel your heart? Is it not cold as ice? Have you any fear or sorrow? Do you repent of any thing?"

"You have only made my heart to cease beating, but I still have it in my breast, and so has Hezekiel, who told me you had deceived us both. You are not the man who, unperceived and without danger, could tear the heart from the breast; it would require witchcraft on your part."

"But I assure you," cried Michel, angrily, "you and Hezekiel and all the rich people, who have sold themselves to me, have hearts as cold as yours, and their real hearts I have here in my chamber."

"Ah! how glibly you can tell lies," said Peter, laughing, "you must tell that to another to be believed; think you I have not seen such tricks by dozens in my journeys? Your hearts in the chamber are made of wax; you're a rich fellow I grant, but you are no magician."

Now the giant was enraged and burst open the chamber door, saying, "Come in and read all the labels and look yonder is Peter Munk's heart; do you see how it writhes? Can that too be of wax?"

"For all that, it is of wax," replied Peter. "A genuine heart does not writhe like that. I have mine still in my breast. No! you are no magician."

"But I will prove it to you," cried the former angrily. "You shall feel that it is your heart." He took it, opened Peter's waistcoat, took the stone from his breast, and held it up. Then taking the heart, he breathed on it, and set it carefully in its proper place, and immediately Peter felt how it beat, and could rejoice again. "How do you feel now?" asked Michel, smiling.

"True enough, you were right," replied Peter, taking carefully the little cross from his pocket. "I should never have believed such things could be done."

"You see I know something of witchcraft, do I not? But, come, I will now replace the stone again."

"Gently, Herr Michel," cried Peter, stepping backwards, and holding up the cross, "mice are caught with bacon, and this time you have been deceived;" and immediately he began to repeat the prayers that came into his mind.

Now Michel became less and less, fell to the ground, and writhed like a worm, groaning and moaning, and all the hearts round began to beat, and became convulsed, so that it sounded like a clock maker's workshop.

Peter was terrified, his mind was quite disturbed; he ran from the house, and, urged by the anguish of the moment, climbed up a steep rock, for he heard Michel get up, stamping and raving, and denouncing curses on him. When he reached the top, he ran towards the Tannenbuehl; a dreadful thunder-storm came on; lightning flashed around him, splitting the trees, but he reached the precincts of the glass-manikin in safety.

His heart beat joyfully--only because it did beat; but now he looked back with horror on his past life, as he did on the thunderstorm that was destroying the beautiful forest on his right and left. He thought of his wife, a beautiful, good woman, whom he had murdered from avarice; he appeared to himself an outcast from mankind, and wept bitterly as he reached the hill of the glass-manikin.

The Schatzhauser was sitting under a pine-tree, and was smoking a small pipe; but he looked more serene than before.

"Why do you weep, Peter?" asked he, "have you not recovered your heart? Is the cold one still in your breast?"

"Alas! sir," sighed Peter, "when I still carried about with me the cold stony heart, I never wept, my eyes were as dry as the ground in July; but now my old heart will almost break with what have done. I have driven my debtors to misery, set the dogs on the sick and poor, and you yourself know how my whip fell upon her beautiful forehead."

"Peter, you were a great sinner," said the little man. "Money and idleness corrupted you, until your heart turned to stone, and no longer knew joy, sorrow, repentance, or compassion. But repentance reconciles; and if I only knew that you were truly sorry for your past life, it might yet be in my power to do something for you."

"I wish nothing more," replied Peter, dropping his head sorrowfully. "It is all over with me, I can no more rejoice in my lifetime; what shall I do thus alone in the world? My mother will never pardon me for what I have done to her, and I have perhaps brought her to the grave, monster that I am! Elizabeth, my wife, too,--rather strike me dead, Herr Schatzhauser, then my wretched life will end at once."

"Well," replied the little man, "if you wish nothing else, you can have it, so my ax is at hand." He quietly took his pipe from his mouth, knocked the ashes out, and put it into his pocket. Then rising slowly, he went behind the pines. But Peter sat down weeping in the grass, his life had no longer any value for him, and he patiently awaited the deadly blow. After a short time, he heard gentle steps behind him, and thought, "Now he is coming."

"Look up once more, Peter Munk," cried the little man. He wiped the tears from his eyes and looked up, and beheld his mother, and Elizabeth his wife, who kindly gazed on him. Then he jumped up joyfully, saying, "You are not dead, then, Elizabeth, nor you, mother; and have you forgiven me?"

"They will forgive you," said the glass-manikin, "because you feel true repentance, and all shall be forgotten. Go home now, to your father's hut, and be a charcoal-burner as before; if you are active and honest, you will do credit to your trade, and your neighbors will love and esteem you more than if you possessed ten tons of gold." Thus saying, the glass-manikin left them. The three praised and blessed him, and went home.

The splendid house of wealthy Peter stood no longer; it was struck by lightning, and burnt to the ground, with all its treasures. But they were not far from his father's hut, and thither they went, without caring much for their great loss. But what was their surprise when they reached the hut; it was changed into a handsome farm-house, and all in it was simple, but good and cleanly.

"This is the glass-manikin's doing," cried Peter.

"How beautiful!" said Frau Elizabeth; "and here I feel more at home than in the larger house, with many servants."

Henceforth Peter Munk became an industrious and honest man. He was content with what he had, carried on his trade cheerfully, and thus it was that he became wealthy by his own energy, and respected and beloved in the whole forest. He no longer quarreled with his wife, but honored his mother, and relieved the poor who came to his door. When, after twelvemonths, Fran Elizabeth presented him with a beautiful little boy, Peter went to the Tannenbuehl, and repeated the verse as before. But the glass-manikin did not show himself.

"Mr. Schatzhauser," he cried loudly, "only listen to me. I wish nothing but to ask you to stand godfather to my little son." But he received no answer, and only a short gust of wind rushed through the pines, and cast a few cones on the grass.

"Then I will take these as a remembrance, as you will not show yourself," cried Peter, and he put them in his pocket, and returned home. But when he took off his jacket, and his mother turned out the pockets before putting it away, four large rolls of money fell out; and when they opened them, they found them all good and new Baden dollars, and not one counterfeit, and these were the intended godfather's gift for little Peter, from the little man in the Tannenbuehl. Thus they lived on, quietly and cheerfully; and many a time Peter Munk, when gray-headed, would say, "It is indeed better to be content with little, than to have wealth and a cold heart."

THE DWARF AND THE TWINS
SNOW WHITE AND ROSE RED
Treasures Retold 1

Once upon a time in a world where magic and technology collide with unexpected consequences…

When Martin helps a pregnant woman to flee from the king's men, he doesn't know that the twins she bears will change his solitary life forever.

What if the Brother's Grimm misunderstood the dwarf in the original tale of "Snow White and Rose Red"?

The book includes a bonus story and the original fairy tale.

ISBN 978-3-95681-028-2
auch als eBook erhältlich

Leave your eMail address so I can inform you about new releases, and this book will arrive as an eBook in your Inbox shortly after

http://www.katharinagerlach.com/readers

ROYAL SWANS
THE SEVEN SWANS
Treasuers Retold 7

Once upon a time in a world where magic and technology collide with unexpected consequences…

When neighboring royals visit the kingdom, Prince Laurent declines the princess' advances with dire consequences. Turned into swans, he and his brothers flee, followed by their sister in a flying machine. But then, they crash-land on a cemetery. Can they regain their humanity before the enraged princess catches up with them? And what about the strange ghost Laurent feels drawn to?

What if Hans Christian Andersen overlooked "The Seven Swans" part in breaking the curse?

The book includes a bonus story and the original fairy tale.

ISBN 978-3-95681-074-9
also available as eBook